MIAMI
The Veng

MIAN

"MIAMI VICE is the series that is blowing standard television out of the water."

Rolling Stone

"The coolest and most contemporary of cop shows."

USA Today

"The most talked about dramatic series in the television industry since 'Hill Street Blues.'"

The New York Times

"The best new cop show of the season and possibly the best new drama, period."

Los Angeles Daily News

"The best... vigor and street realism and two interestingly shaded detectives as unstoppable heroes."

Ellery Queen Mystery Magazine

Don't miss—

MIAMI VICE #1 *The Florida Burn*

Other Avon Books by
Stephen Grave

MIAMI VICE #1: THE FLORIDA BURN

THE VENGEANCE GAME

A novel by

STEPHEN GRAVE

Based on the Universal Television Series
MIAMI VICE
Created by Anthony Yerkovich
Adapted from the episodes "Hit List"
Written by Joel Surnow
and "Calderone's Dream"
Written by Joel Surnow & Alfonse Ruggiero, Jr.

AVON
PUBLISHERS OF BARD, CAMELOT, DISCUS AND FLARE BOOKS

MIAMI VICE #2: THE VENGEANCE GAME is an original publication of Avon Books. This work has never before appeared in book form.

AVON BOOKS
A division of
The Hearst Corporation
1790 Broadway
New York, New York 10019

Published by arrangement with MCA Publishing Rights, a Division of MCA Inc.
Library of Congress Catalog Card Number: 85-90678
ISBN: 0-380-89931-0

First Avon Printing, November 1985

Printed in the U. S. A.

WFH 10 9 8 7 6 5 4 3 2 1

For
John Brillhart
the better looking half
of the Tom and John Comedy Hour

vice: moral depravity or corruption; habitual, abnormal behavior patterns detrimental to health or usefulness; sexual immorality, especially prostitution.

vice squad: police squad charged with enforcement of laws concerning gambling, pornography, prostitution, and the illegal use of liquor and narcotics.

—1—

THE *deal is goin' down,* thought Esteban Barrencia, nervously adding, *or is it?* Rudolpho Mendez was due to materialize for some serious verbal swap in one minute, thirty-two seconds according to Barrencia's fourteen-thousand-dollar gold Rolex. The subject of their conversation would be sixty keys of laboratory-pure, snow-white nose candy—enough cocaine to perform hot-dogging ski tricks on. A cool two-million, four-hundred-thousand dollars' worth, enough to keep the brain-damaged high schoolers in Liberty City free-basing until the turn of the century. Barrencia knew Mendez would try to put the haggling screws to him, and grind him down to a price tag of one-million-nine, or thirty-two grand a key. He was prepared to settle out at thirty-four. It was all gravy anyway. Barrencia had been holding *this* particular stash of imported Colombian coke for a considerable piece of time.

Barrencia sniffled and rubbed his large-pored nose with the back of his hand. The guy standing across from him in the Starliner Towers Hilton elevator pretended he did not exist. Barrencia shoved his hands into his pockets and assessed the man.

The guy was maybe five-ten barefoot and mildly handsome in an introspective, scholarly way. He wore a modest corduroy jacket over a pastel sport shirt open at the throat. Behind the frames of his steel-rimmed glasses, the man's blue eyes seemed to sparkle with some inner joke. A high school history teacher, thought Barrencia. Tousled brown hair, medium-cut. A real crowd face, good-looking but nothing you'd see on the cover of *Gentleman's Quarterly*. Sort of Clark Kent–ish. Lean-looking. Probably works out three times a week in a gym. Barrencia shifted his stance and sucked in his gut. A little too much of the high life the coke trade could bring had rendered him flabby and toneless.

Well, señor professor, he thought defensively, *I could buy and sell your entire family for three generations in each direction for what I earn running coke in a month. Shove that in your briefcase*. The guy was probably down in Miami on his annual six-day vacation—coach fare, cheap meals, the whole tourist package. Barrencia made it a rule to devote one hour of each business day to business, and the remaining time to pleasure. *Put that in your imitation meerschaum and smoke it, mister schoolteacher!*

The elevator bell chimed softly, and the burnished

doors rolled back to admit Barrencia to the twenty-second floor. His overpriced watch told him he, at least, was right on time. He left the American, and whatever dull life-story he possessed, behind in the elevator.

He pulled the room key to Suite 2010 from his coat pocket as he walked to the door. Mendez was not loitering in the hallway; the next step would be to phone him.

He locked the door behind him out of habit and dumped his coat on the desk. The dope he was about to sell Mendez was downstairs in the subbasement parking garage—stashed in the trunk of a rented Cadillac Seville. When Mendez flashed the cash, Barrencia would hand over three keys—one for the trunk and two for the suitcases inside—and reveal *which* of the hundred and fifty cars in the garage held the treasure. Then it would be party time.

Barrencia had planned that, too. He thought about it as he switched on the color TV, which came to life right in the middle of some R-rated movie on the building's private cable. Some buff dude gigged out in a punk fatigue jacket and chained boots was marching through a police station, an Uzi submachine gun in one hand and a pump-style riot shotgun in the other, singlehandedly decimating every cop in sight. It was the middle of the night, and the dude was wearing shades and killing cops. The scene gave Barrencia a reassuring glow inside. You only killed cops, he thought, when you couldn't buy them. And cops could be bought for a bargain price in Miami. Metro officers weren't paid doodley.

Mendez was late. That was okay, Barrencia knew,

because coke dealers functioned on a different time scale from normal beings; maybe it was all the chemical intake. Barrencia never got high on his own supply—though if someone *else* had the party favors, he was willing and enthusiastic. But since Mendez was late, Barrencia decided to whistle up some Room Service champagne to toast the deal. It wouldn't do for Mendez to think Barrencia cheap. This guy could be a solid future customer, and Barrencia liked that kind just fine—especially since he was starting to expand his little enterprise. He was coming up in the world, and could afford to spring for a split or two of bubbly.

He yanked the phone from its cradle and punched the proper buttons. "Hey, Room Service?" He said Room *Sorviss:* he hadn't quite Americanized his accent even after six years in Miami. "I need two bottles of Taittinger 1976 Blanc de Blancs, and six flutes." Barrencia never drank champagne out of the same glass twice, thus the request for extra glasses. There was to be only himself and Mendez. "Hurry it up, please."

Mendez was five minutes late.

Barrencia turned up the sound and watched the mayhem for a few minutes. A sharp, officious rap came at the door. That wouldn't be Mendez—not *knock-knock-knock*. Barrencia had spent enough time in hotels to recognize the sound of Room Service.

He glanced out the door's glass peephole long enough to see the serving cart and the white-jacketed attendant. He yanked back the bolt and disengaged the sliding chain lock as well. (His old paranoid habits, he estimated, would only die when he did.)

He turned the knob and was about to open the door when it flew toward him violently, smacking his face and breaking his nose. The world rolled sideways, and he took three stumbling backward steps. He did not fall. His gun hand reflexively darted to grab the .45 automatic holstered snugly beneath his left armpit, under the coat.

Barrencia's vision focused as he heard the door thump shut. He saw the schoolteacher type from the elevator and instantly registered two odd things about him. First: the man was wearing waiter's whites over his sport coat; the ensemble was bulky and ill-fitting, unlike Barrencia's tailored clothing. Second: a pistol was aimed unwaveringly at Barrencia's solar plexus. His own gun was only halfway out. He continued his draw even though he had no hope.

The stranger's eyes still laughed. His pistol was a Colt .45 revolver with a fat black silencer seated on the business end of the long barrel. It looked like a black toilet-tissue tube. When the gun discharged, it made a coughing noise like a firm handclap—*kunk!*

The scooped-out slug caught Barrencia in the chest and lifted him from the floor. It tore a large exit wound and penetrated the sliding glass balcony doors behind him. The closed curtains rustled as the flattened bullet perforated them and broke the glass.

The impact made him forget about his own gun, and the slam of agony landed him on his back, on the floor.

The stranger stepped closer. His expression had

not changed. He saw everything—Barrencia gasping for air, his eyes dimming, the gore pumping from his chest—but none of it affected his calm and businesslike manner. The eyes still laughed silently; the mouth seemed ready to turn upward in a smile, as though the man had eavesdropped on someone else's joke.

Barrencia struggled to say *why*. He could not draw breath. His chest was a block of ice; he needed air and could not pull it in. Something was wrong with his lungs. They were gone, and he was going to die.

He would have done all the usual things—fought, begged, offered money, played for time—but the stranger leaned closer, put the fat barrel an inch away from Barrencia's forehead, and pulled the trigger again.

Barrencia's last thought was that the assassin was very smart. The use of a revolver meant no shell casings would be left behind as evidence.

The second slug did the trick. The stranger lingered long enough to empty the gun anyway. After Barrencia's body stopped the remaining four bullets, it was the deadest thing in Miami.

The stranger broke the silencer from the pistol and put both into a brown paper bag he'd pulled from his back pocket. Then he wiped the doorknob to Suite 2010 with a towel and locked the door behind him.

Barrencia's body would be discovered by the Room Service waiter. The Dade County coroner would be moved to remark that the killing was particularly savage even for a drug-related murder. The killer had continued firing long after the victim was dead meat.

Somebody, it would be surmised, was trying to make a point.

The two suitcases full of cocaine in the subbasement remained unclaimed until the rental agency picked up the car.

–2–

JAMES "Sonny" Crockett stared at his face in the steamy bathroom mirror. He had white foam artistically smeared all over his face and looked like a deranged Santa Claus. *Adios, compadre,* he thought . . . and the disposable razor cut its first swath through the foam. He kept one ear perked for the transmission coming from the next room: the sounds copied through with the tinny, unenhanced characteristics of reception from a discreetly planted surveillance bug. It was a sound Sonny's mind automatically compensated for.

"*. . . eat your breakfast; it's getting cold . . .*" Female voice.

Then a male one, obviously on the phone: "*. . . yes, we're down here in the balmy sunshine . . .*"

Sonny's habitually effected three-day growth of

beard parted company with his face. Having bare skin on his chin would come as a shock.

Him, now off the phone: *"This is the life, huh?"*

Her: *"So what's on the big agenda for today, hmm?"* There was a trace of bored sarcasm in her voice.

Him: *"Goin' uptown. You and I gotta meet some people in Lauderdale—so get some sun today."*

Her, after an icy pause: *"What's that supposed to mean?"*

Him, after an equally cold beat, snapping back in a calm voice: *"It means I don't want important people thinking I'm married to a corpse fresh outta the meat freezer."*

Sonny snorted and dunked his razor. "Never let it be said that coke dealers aren't the epitome of charm."

A chuckle came back at him from the living room of the expensive, soft-tech condo. Ricardo Tubbs sat on a leather footstool near the balcony windows. To his right a TEAC tape recorder with ten-inch reels cranked slowly away at 3¾ inches per second, immortalizing Felix Castronova's snotty morning rap. Tubbs, nursing his third cup of coffee, was dressed in his usual light coat and silk shirt—natty, neat, smelling of Baron cologne.

Tubbs put his eye to the tripod-mounted, high-powered binoculars that were aimed through a crack in the balcony curtains. The vision circles took in the eleventh-floor penthouse of the building across the street, where Castronova and his wife were doing the breakfast bit.

"That's criminal," said Tubbs in the direction of

the bathroom. "I'd *never* mistake a bit of trim like that for a dead body."

As if in response, Susan Castronova's voice continued: *"Maybe I feel like a corpse! I'm still not sure why we had to leave New Jersey to come to this dump."*

"Hah! A woman after your own heart, Tubbs!"

"Amen," said Tubbs.

"Two million extra per annum a good enough reason, sweetheart?" Castronova said the term of endearment with little affection. *"Florida is the land of opportunity."*

Tubbs rolled his eyes. These two were going to goof around forever, swapping banal chatter. He loosened the drag on the tripod and scanned the rest of the honeycomb of balconies across the street. On a twelfth-floor breezeway he sighted a sweet young thing just barely inside a string bikini that clung like paint to her aerobically enhanced curves. Her breasts struggled to burst free of the skimpy top. She had just come from the twelfth-floor pool. Long, glossy damp hair. Tubbs' imagination concocted an aroma for it. Her body was lithe, pantherlike, and her soft tan was evenly distributed. She was a tasty item. Unescorted. Tubbs tracked with her as she strolled along the breezeway. On a whim, his hand moved to the surveillance camera on the anchor mount below the binocs. He focused on the young woman and snapped off a shot for his collection. "Mm-mm," he mused happily, "the upside of surveillance."

"Big deal," said Susan Castronova. The VU me-

ters on the tape deck jumped in time with her voice. *"Business—always business."*

Tubbs' attention wandered back to the bikinied beauty just as she was embraced from behind by a sixty-five-year-old swingled-out sugar daddy. She purred and rubbed against him. The coffee went sour in Tubbs' stomach.

"Unless I inherit about fifteen million dollars," he said to Sonny, "I don't stand a chance in this town."

But then, he reflected, how many gorgeous women wandered around Brooklyn wearing technically nothing?

Moreover, how many ex-New York street cops were able to salvage their law enforcement careers by hooking up, as he had, with the crack Vice unit of Dade County, Florida—gateway to the cocaine trade of the universe? Two months ago he'd been flying by the seat of his pants on forged identity, footing his bills with counterfeit cash skimmed from his New York connections. Down here he'd hooked up with Sonny Crockett—and an odder couple would be hard to imagine, at first review. Sonny, it turned out, was hungry to bust the Colombian dope dealer who had offed Tubbs' brother, Rafael, back in the Big Apple. Two minds, one cause. Tubbs had lost his brother, Crockett had lost his partner—both because of Francisco Calderone, a millionaire by virtue of the cocaine trade. Calderone made Castronova, who was a mid-range, Yuppie-type dealer, look like a grade-school kid.

Calderone had forty-two million dollars' worth of grease, and so had slipped past Crockett and

Tubbs despite their best efforts to play the game legally. He had fled back to the Caribbean—or wherever it was he holed up—after jumping two million dollars bail. He'd shrugged off more bread than Tubbs could earn in most of his life.

The whole affair was a badly busted flush. But it had snared Tubbs a heavy recommendation from Crockett's boss, Lou Rodriguez. Time had passed. Tubbs forgot his native New York and had become part of Miami Vice—the ease with which his life had changed was unsettling, but he thought about that less these days. He left behind no family of note; no girl friends. . . . But Sonny had proven a good friend and a professional partner. All told, he had little to worry about this week, except the injustice of the bikinied lovely paying so much attention to the gross, droopy, dyspeptic high roller across the way. The only thing his pants were full of was cool green cash.

Of course, Susan Castronova was no car wreck, either. Tubbs shifted the high-powered lenses back and focused on the spot where her bathrobe drooped open.

"Well, what do you think?" said Sonny, buttoning up a crisp white dress shirt. "Do I look like a guy who's about to get himself a divorce?"

"I didn't know they still called it divorce," Tubbs said, not looking. "Except in that stupid song."

"Tammy Wynette is not stupid," Crockett groused, picking up their buddy-buddy argument. "When are you gonna learn that there are only two types of real music in the world, Tubbs?"

"Two?"

"Yeah—country and western."

"The man with the blade-sharp wit," Tubbs countered. He turned around and nearly went into shock. Crockett wasn't wearing his normal football jersey or cartoon T-shirt. He was putting on a *tie*. He actually knew how to knot one. His ragout blond-brown hair was *combed*. "You *shaved,*" said Tubbs with quiet awe, then admiration. "You definitely look like you're on the way up, my man. Told you that hanging around me would be good for you."

Sonny clutched at his heart. "Lie to me, lie to me some more!"

Tubbs made a circle with his thumb and forefinger. "A-okay." Crockett, in this state, could almost pass for a young, upwardly mobile urban defense attorney.

Crockett punched in a tie pin.

"Little touch o' gold looks good on a man," said Tubbs.

"What happened to the battling Bickersons?"

Tubbs nodded toward the window. "She went inside. Maid cleared away the breakfast stuff."

There was a thumping on the door of their room. That would be Ernest Switek, thought Tubbs; he always knocked too many times. Funny, how he'd gotten to know these guys with such speed. Switek would be wearing a loud aloha shirt, untucked, and canvas pants. He'd lumber in like a bearded bear, probably carrying a box of jelly doughnuts. Switek's partner, Tommy Ray Zito, would be wearing a gray T-shirt with a crumpled pack of smokes in the sleeve. Skintight corduroys and jogging shoes. Zito was whipcord-skinny and had that slightly oily dealer look to him; he'd be chomping on a toothpick or sucking on an unlit butt. He'd have five o'clock shadow and pimples on his chin. Switek and Zito got along well in the vice squad not because they were any Dick Tracys, but because, based on their appearance, nobody would ever suspect them of being cops.

"Caroline'll beg you to come back to her when she sees the real Sonny," Tubbs said as Crockett answered the door. "No lie."

Switek and Zito rolled in. Tubbs' prediction had been nearly one hundred percent correct.

"Hiya girls," said Sonny.

"Hooya, hooya," boomed Switek. "How's Angelique? Did you miss us, honeypot?"

Tubbs grinned. "Angelique" was a foldout that Switek pinned up every time they pulled a surveillance assignment, which could sometimes drag on for weeks, even months. She was a statuesque blonde, long-legged and silicone-injected, and her picture had come out of one of those magazines found in the NO ONE UNDER 21 YEARS OF AGE section at the local smoke shop. Angelique, over a stretch of time, had become a third member of the usual two-cop stakeout routine.

"She missed you, Switek. I can tell," said Tubbs.

"Who the hell is *this?*" said Zito, cocking his thumb exaggeratedly at Sonny.

Switek gave Sonny a once-over. "Smooth-looking dude. You trying to make time with Angelique, hot pants?"

Tubbs said, "This guy wandered in here claiming

to be one James Sonny Crockett. Didn't fool me for a microsecond."

"My god, he *shaved,*" said Zito with something akin to awe.

"All right, all right, why don't you two reprobates do your jobs?" Sonny lifted his jacket off a chair back and slung it over his shoulder.

"And what's new with America's favorite couple?" said Switek, setting down his box. Tubbs noted with amusement that it contained bear claws, not jelly doughnuts.

"Nada." Tubbs checked the binoculars again: nothing new. "Castronova's being pretty tight-lipped about how he's setting up shop. Barely talks to his own wife about it. She's bored catatonic by the whole thing."

"The jaded *nuevo*-rich," said Zito. "God save us." He poked a cigarette into his face and lit a wooden match by snapping it against his thumbnail. He reached into a paper sack and pulled out his Cokes. Zito consumed two six-packs of Coca-Cola daily to maintain his caffeine high. If his head began to throb, he crunched up three or four Excedrin tablets dry and washed them down with the fizzy brown stuff.

"We have a loose tail set up down on Brickle—about three blocks short," said Crockett. "Just in case he decides to make a move."

Tubbs and Crockett's surveillance, which had absorbed most of the night uneventfully, was now over for another twelve hours. Felix Castronova was just barely big enough to bust. But like other fish in the drug trade, he'd begun to broaden his horizons recently. His connections reached higher. And Dade Metro Vice was setting up for a sweeping bust of middle-range coke dealers at the behest of Lou Rodriguez—something to give the mayor around election time, to justify their existence. Castronova and his *compadres*, collected in one crosstown assault, would net enough of a drug haul to merit a mention on the evening news—broadcast under the slug line, *the biggest local drug haul in the history of Miami Beach*.

It was grindingly routine, like making arrest quotas. Nothing like chasing Calderone, who pulled down in excess of a hundred million, tax-free, every two years. But without middlemen like Castronova, Calderone's empire would not exist—nor would the drug fiefdoms of dozens of other big-league scum like him.

Switek and Zito settled in. Switek switched on the tube with half a bear claw in his mush; Zito made for the bathroom to relieve himself of his two morning Cokes. He handed Crockett's toilet kit out to him.

"Have a ball, guys," said Sonny, tossing them a small salute and grandly letting Tubbs precede him out the door. Their exit was accomplished with considerably more style than was Switek and Zito's entrance.

Chomping and swallowing, Switek leaned forward and socketed his eye to the binoculars. Susan Castronova was alone on the balcony across the way, dressed in a loose, wafting blouse and designer jeans.

"Hey . . . uh, Zito?"

Zito's voice echoed off the bathroom tiles from behind the half-closed door. "Yeah?"

"She takin' off her shirt! Omigod, she's naked!"

Zito came crashing out of the can with his pants at half-mast, wrestling the zipper and trying to stump across the room to the window. His legs double-crossed, and he tumbled to the carpeting with a thump.

Switek didn't look up from the binoculars. "You're gonna hurt yourself, y'know, rushing out like that. Get a rupture or something . . ."

Zito crawled to his knees and shoved Switek aside. He squinted through the lenses. "What are you talking about, man?"

All innocence, Switek checked again. There was no one on the balcony. "Whoops. Sorry, amigo—you missed it. She was bucky-tail naked, right there."

Zito narrowed his eyes at Switek, and without a word popped open a Coke and sat down to watch *Superman III*.

"You have to learn to look on the bright side of things, Sonny," Tubbs began as they cut through the morning traffic in Crockett's confiscated '84 Corvette—a replacement, by way of the impound yard, for a similar Corvette Sonny had torn to smithereens a few weeks back in order to keep Tubbs from getting filled with bullets. Crockett's standard cover for vice assignments was "Sonny T. Burnett." Along with his fancy car, he possessed a one-hundred-thousand-dollar cigarette speedboat and a forty-foot sloop docked at the marina—all confiscated goods. Pushers and dope dealers lived well;

and when they were shipped away for prison sentences, they left behind expensive cars, expensive clothes, and expensive living quarters—all of which Dade Metro Vice distributed among its officers. There was no other way to pull off the sham of elaborate wealth in order to suck the bona fide dealers into the net. Tubbs was looking forward to some of these job benefits himself, once he'd been a Miami resident awhile longer.

But there was the flip side of that costly coin. Sonny was also the father of a six-year-old son, Billy, whom he had to steal time to see. His work with the vice unit, often requiring weeks or months undercover to set up elaborate sting operations, had jammed a depth charge into his marriage to an upstanding, honey-blond lady named Caroline. Thus the spiff-up, prior to this morning's bill of fare, which happened to be more legal arm wrestling with lawyers over what Tammy Wynette called D-I-V-O-R-C-E.

"What the hell is the bright side of divorce, dark meat?" Sonny snapped from behind his tinted Vuarnets. The Corvette's top was down, and smoke from Sonny's cigarette trailed backward in the slipstream of warm Miami air.

"At least it ain't root canal, white bread," Tubbs shot back, and they both laughed. There was little mirth in what Sonny was preparing to do, but he had not abandoned his rueful sense of humor, which was a good sign. Tubbs didn't have the full portfolio in mind yet, but he knew one thing from his discussions with Sonny: Sonny loved Caroline. And

Caroline loved him. But the marriage wasn't pumping healthily away because of the job. End of discussion.

"I know, I know, I gotta have a sense of humor about these things. Right?" They were approaching the county courthouse. "Oh, Christ, I think I see Janet."

Tubbs squinted ahead.

"Janet Buckley. My attorney. At law."

"Oh."

Crockett curbed the Corvette, and he and Tubbs switched places. Crockett waved at Janet Buckley, a trim woman in her late thirties dressed in businesslike lawyer attire and simple—therefore expensive—jewelry. The impression she left was one of understated power. She smiled a lot at Sonny, but Sonny had never seen her smile while negotiating. If his budding romance with Gina Calabrese—another officer working for Metro Vice—panned to nothing, maybe there was some potential in Janet. But Crockett thought not. He would never be able to erase the mental image of her as the woman who helped dismantle his marriage to Caroline.

Tubbs saw Crockett spot the yellow Volvo parked thirty yards away. Caroline's car. The car she took Billy to school in. He saw Crockett's face tighten.

"Hey, on the square," he said, meeting Crockett's eyes directly, "you need anything, I'm here."

Crockett squeezed Tubbs' bicep. "Thanks, partner."

"You got it." Tubbs straightened the stick and

moved into traffic. In the rearview he saw Crockett link up with Janet Buckley.

He was many blocks away, at Tenth and Lejeune, when he got the emergency call on the police-band radio.

–3–

"CAR'S *on its way up, Mister C. . . .*"

"Now where are you going?" Susan Castronova's voice complained via the surveillance link. Switek made a fey expression, mocking her.

Castronova said, *"Teddy's gonna fit me for a couple of suits. Hey, I'll be back in an hour—"*

"Can I come?"

"You just stay here and keep it warm, huh?"

Polishing off his last bear claw and blasting it down with a slug of lukewarm coffee, Switek said, "Don't these friggin' dealers ever do anything but buy clothes?"

"Yeah," said Zito, sucking his Coke can dry. "They buy cars."

"Tail car number one, start your engine," Switek said into his throat mike. Then, in a jokey tone: "He's going to the tailor today!"

Tilting the binoculars, Switek saw a black stretch limo wheel up to the basement garage bay. A parking valet wearing a red jacket got out of the driver's door.

"Felix, I want to buy some parachute pants like these." Switek tilted back. Castronova's wife was showing him a picture in some fashion magazine.

"I catch you wearing parachute pants, sugar-bunny, I'll throw you out of an airplane."

"Joe Charming lives," said Zito.

A blond surfer type with muscles crowding his other muscles stepped onto the balcony. One of Castronova's beefcake bodyguards, obviously. They trooped back into the penthouse.

Below, near the parking garage, the valet stripped off his red coat and mopped his brow. It was already near eighty degrees. He tossed the coat into the front seat of the limousine.

Switek shifted to the front doors of the building, waiting for Castronova and his watchdog to emerge. He did not see the parking valet pull a leather case from his back pocket and insert two mini-earplugs into his ears. He adjusted his rectangular steel-rimmed glasses, and leaned against the limo to wait.

Felix Castronova and Bruce Blodgett, his surfer bodyguard, cut across the lobby of the building after leaving the elevators. Blodgett was packing a fully loaded .44-caliber AutoMag under his windbreaker. That gun would blow apart a runaway semi, Castronova thought—but he still had a small .32-caliber Walther PPK in his ankle holster. A little backup never hurt.

Outside the automatic glass doors, Blodgett signaled the valet to bring the limousine. Castronova looked around for his other bodyguard. "Where the hell is Nickie?"

"He had to go to the can," said Blodgett. "Should be out in a second."

The valet straightened his cap and tooled the limousine to the curb. Jumping out smartly, he held the door for Castronova.

"Tip him, Bruce," Castronova said.

Bruce dug out a five-dollar bill and pressed it into the valet's hand. The valet smiled slightly and folded the bill into his shirt pocket, saying nothing. He had, Blodgett noticed, very clear blue eyes. They almost seemed to sparkle. He climbed into the limousine after Castronova.

The valet reached into the front seat for his jacket. The jacket was an ill fit because the real valet— the one bound and gagged in the parking basement—had been a slight man, shorter and thinner than the man with the steel-rimmed glasses. He moved the jacket aside and closed his right hand around the pistol grip of a Remington 12-gauge automatic riot shotgun. There was already a shell in the chamber.

In a single swift and unstoppable motion, he brought the truncated bore of the weapon level with the passenger window and fired four rounds without blinking. The first shot blew the dark-tinted glass inward. Castronova and Blodgett twitched and danced in the backseat. The next shot caught Blodgett in the chest and head and tore him apart, spraying pieces of him all around the plush cabin. Castronova died groping for his own gun, his designer clothing peppered with fresh blood. The fourth shot was for good measure, for cleanup, for just-in-case, even though the assassin knew both men were history. Gray smoke drifted from the blown-in window. Proudly, the assassin noted that not a single shotgun pellet had dented the hide of the car. He had delivered full value through the passenger window.

Then, annoyingly, someone behind him was shouting.

Switek dropped his empty coffee cup on the floor. "They just hit him!" he screamed into the microphone.

Zito was already up and moving, his Magnum dancing in its shoulder holster as he made for the door.

"Go! Go!" Switek snatched up the riot gun leaning against the door and chased Zito out. They had over ten floors to race down before they got to the street level. Nobody had expected a shootout, and there were only the officers in the chase car, three blocks away.

"Drop it!" Nickie yelled, his voice cracking. "Drop it now!"

The assassin knew there was a handgun pointed at his spine. He chucked the riot gun into the limousine through the broken window. It landed with a soft thud on the carnage inside. Slowly he turned, with his hands in the air. His expression had not changed.

Nickie was young and wiry, and he held a gun the assassin recognized as a Browning 9-millimeter automatic that held a seven-shot clip. He held the pistol in a professional firing stance.

A small smile creased across the assassin's face, as though he were in complete control of the situation despite the reality of the weapon pointed at him.

"You stay right there!" Nickie shouted. "Keep your hands up and get away from the car!"

At a school in the middle of the Arizona desert, the assassin had learned a very interesting life-saving technique. The school was run by a totally paranoid ex-Ranger who slept wearing a shoulder holster and had a loaded gun within easy reach at any location inside his home. He had trained government agents and mercenaries. He made a living teaching men how to duck, roll, and execute a rapid-fire four-shot routine that put two bullets into the trunk of an aggressor, followed by two to the head.

Nickie seemed ready to explode. The assassin remained utterly unruffled. Nickie edged toward the limousine and tried to get a look inside. Any sudden movement on the part of the assassin would initiate a progression in Nickie's mind whereby he would decide whether to shoot.

In short, Nickie's reaction would not be instantaneous.

The assassin held his arms in the air for half a beat longer, then dropped both hands down in a lightning cross draw. His left yanked up his shirt, his right tugged free an automatic loaded with wadcutters. In the time it took Nickie's eyes to bug with recognition, the assassin cut loose four shots. Two in the chest to immobilize, as he had been taught, and two to ensure death. The hair on the back of Nickie's head flew apart, followed by most of what was inside. His own weapon seemed to hang in the air on the end of his hand for an instant. Then he folded up, dead before his body settled on the concrete.

Nickie, the dumb cluck, had never had a chance. He had allowed the audaciousness of a man's drawing a gun while covered to take him by surprise—and that had meant the end of his span on the planet.

The assassin broke the clip from his automatic and tossed it on top of Nickie's corpse. Its purpose had been served. He walked away from the slaughter with his hands in his pockets—like a man taking a stroll to buy a newspaper.

A blue Mercury sedan glided out of the traffic flow and slowed to the curbside. The assassin opened the door and climbed into the passenger side.

The driver, a dark Latino with a drooping mustache and densely dark preppie sunglasses, said nothing to the assassin. He kept eyes front and pulled back into the traffic just as Switek and Zito came piling out of the hotel lobby across the street.

"Shots fired!" Switek shouted into the walkie-talkie unit he held to the side of his head. "Suspect or suspects in blue Mercury sedan heading south on Nineteenth!"

Zito had his gun out, wary of the limousine. No one inside the hotel had worked up the nerve to approach the death car or the human wreckage inside of it.

The chase car, a black-walled Chevy Nova in institutional gray, roared past Switek as he made the call. The chase driver had tacked onto the Mercury. Seconds later, a Dade Metro squad car, flash-bar dazzling, blew past in the wake of the Nova.

"Jesus, Switek, come and take a look at this," Zito said from the obliterated limo window. "Looks kinda like the meatloaf at Nate's . . . uncooked."

"Who the hell would want to bump Castronova? I mean, he isn't worth the trouble of a professional hit, and that's what we got here. See the weapons? Left behind, and not because the shooter was absentminded. They're used up. Even odds says they're totally untraceable."

Zito seated his Magnum back in its holster. "Yeah." Then he displayed his shield to the bravest of the onlookers who were edging nearer the car. "Hey, Miami Vice! Move back now; there ain't nothing to gawk at here, folks. You! Haul it back there. Police."

The mustachioed man noted the appearance of the two chase cars in his rearview mirror and calmly walked the Mercury up to eighty miles per hour. Next to him, the assassin clipped on his shoulder harness.

The chase cars paced him.

He spotted a blind off-ramp and shot across five lanes to take it. WRONG WAY/NO ENTRANCE signs blurred past on either side. A brief flurry of oncoming cars quickly rear-ended one another and thrumped onto the shoulder of the road to get out of the way of the lunatic driver.

Doggedly, the pursuit vehicles followed him the wrong way up the one-way access, soaring around the blind curve of the ramp. When they slowed at the head of the ramp, ducking cars each way, they each took one of the two possible turns.

"Unit Twelve, this is chase Alpha. I think we drew the wrong straw. Over."

"Chase Alpha, this is Unit Twelve. You sure? I don't see a hint of him."

The radio crackled with dead air for a moment. Then: "Victory one-nine, responding to your make, blue Mercury sedan, license number one-one-five-B-forty-six is a rental vehicle leased to a William Warren of Los Angeles. No priors."

"Chase Alpha this is Unit Twelve. He's gone."

"Unit Twelve—he's *gotta* be on your side of the street . . . uh, over."

"This is Unit Twelve—no way, José. Over."

Tubbs patted the dashboard of the grumbling Corvette the way he would stroke a pet dog's head. On the radio, the immortal BB King was punching out "Lucille," the tune after which the black blues god had dubbed his guitar.

"*Speak* to me Lucille!" Tubbs jived along with the radio.

He cruised down Main, scooping up the sights, letting the world catch a glimpse of the one-and-only Ricardo Tubbs. The early afternoon sidewalk was a smorgasbord of feminine pulchritude.

Tubbs caught a red light and stopped his front bumper an inch or so from the crosswalk line. A pair of blow-dried lookers trotted past, hips switching deliciously. They were aware of his attention and played to him, their Danskins and sultry stride summing them up beautifully.

To himself, Tubbs groaned. "Mamas, you are hurting old Rico bad. Should be a law . . ."

He broke off as a cherry-red Mustang convertible, gleaming as though showroom-new, idled to a stop for the light. Its wire-spoked hubs shot chromium highlights off the buildings all around. After a full five seconds of admiring the automobile, Tubbs' eye was arrested by the pilot.

She had a thick mane of streaked ash-blond hair tied in a large cable braid and draped over her left shoulder. There was a fully loaded halter top somewhere under that hair, but Tubbs couldn't see it. The tantalizing illusion was that, but for the fabulous curtain of hair, the woman only a few feet away was Lady Godiva nude. Her face was a perfect Scandinavian sculpture.

The opposing light switched to yellow just as Tubbs saw her. She returned his interested glance with modest approval.

"Ricardo Tubbs at your service," he said immediately. "Seven-nine-five, three-one-oh-two. Call anytime, twenty-four hours a day; I'll sleep in my tuxedo for you, fair one!"

"You're nice," she said. Her voice flowed past a lilt that could kill. "So's your car."

He flashed a billion-watt grin, and a thousand possible responses rushed through his brain all at once.

"Who do you drive it for?" she said, and Tubbs' smile dripped off his face to puddle in humiliation on the floorboards. Before he could summon a rejoinder, she laid her pedal down and the Mustang's powerhouse took it far away fast.

He switched on the police band to check in, and caught the tail end of the bulletin: "*. . . suspect vehicle in the Castronova killing at Flamingo Towers . . .*"

His mouth dropped open. Castronova had been his and Sonny's stakeout! Did she say *killing?*

He snatched up the mike and called in for the details. The blue Mercury had been spotted parked in the lot at the Deseret Motel down near 23rd and LeJeune.

Tubbs was only thirteen blocks away. He stomped on the pedal and whizzed past the Nordic blond cookie in the Mustang, leaving her eating his dust.

Tubbs was getting better at negotiating—and remembering—Miami's streets. He found the Deseret Motel a scant ten minutes after hearing the broadcast.

In the parking lot, two rookies, Metzger and Young by name, had staked out the Mercury. Tubbs jumped out of the Corvette, ran to the squad car, and flashed his shield.

"That was my stakeout at the Flamingo!" Tubbs said, disoriented. "What the hell happened?"

Young spoke first. "It was heavy-duty—three guys wasted right under our noses. Castronova and two of his pet thugs got blown away."

"What about the stakeout?"

Young shrugged. "Two detectives at the scene. Word I got was a parking valet at the Flamingo did the shooting."

Tubbs grumbled to himself. "Parking valet, my

ass. Nobody expected any gunplay. You two the only guys here?"

Metzger climbed out of the patrol car, jacking a round into the chamber of his riot gun as he did. He was itching to do some violence and advance his rank. "We're all there is. Suspect is inside the Deseret. I say we take him before he peeks out the curtains and starts sniping!"

Tubbs reached out and pushed the muzzle of the shotgun away from his middle, where Metzger had inadvertently pointed it while yammering. It would do no good to get shot up on account of these beginners. "No cowboy crap," he said. "We wait for backup."

"It's already called in," said Young, glancing nervously toward the Deseret for the hundredth time. Tubbs saw that this one, at least, wasn't eager for combat; and he was thankful for that. "They're en route."

As if cued, Tubbs heard several sirens Dopplering together in an all-out Code Three. "Idiots!" he snarled. "Why don't we just send the dude a Candy-Gram to let him know the *po*-lice have arrived?" He wrested the shotgun out from Metzger's grasp and tore across the open parking lot.

Metzger and Young stood there looking like two befuddled cartoon characters. As Tubbs raced toward the Deseret, they saw a mustachioed man wearing sunglasses appear at the opposite end of the breezeway. Tubbs' trajectory put him dead between the man and the blue Mercury, which was parked in front of the suspect room.

The man with the sunglasses did not take long

to make up his mind. He turned and ran, realizing that reaching his room or his car was impossible. Tubbs spotted him and gave chase. Metzger and Young headed for the room.

The fugitive bashed through the nearest exit door, which was still swinging shut on its hydraulic closure when Tubbs came to it. He moved through barrel-first, but gunfire did not fill up the doorway. Apparently his quarry was no longer up for shooting. The tail of his coat wisped around another corner at the end of the next passageway just as Tubbs came through the door.

"Halt! Police!" So much for the standard warning.

Tubbs pumped after him, eating up the distance like a track star, sucking air nasally as he ran. He slid around the corner with his shotgun ready to cut loose . . . and heard a woman scream.

She was screaming at the sight of Tubbs' shotgun. He had burst out into the middle of pedestrian traffic on the busy eastbound boulevard. Shoppers and joggers jumped out of the way, thinking Tubbs was some sort of gun-toting lunatic. Several drivers on the street craned their heads to look. A Mercedes rear-ended a Volkswagen bug, and there was the tinkle of smashed safety glass.

Angered, Tubbs yelled into the face of the wailing woman who had frozen to the sidewalk in front of him—while other citizens dumped their packages and dove and jostled for cover. "I'm a police officer, dammit. It's okay!" He fumbled for his badge while looking up and down the clogged street for his prey.

The man with the mustache and sunglasses was gone.

Defeated, Tubbs made sure the shotgun barrel was pointed up, then slogged back toward the motel. Metzger huffed up behind him. Seeing the confused people milling about, he asked, "Geez, what did you do, shoot the guy?"

"No," said Tubbs, "just showed my face without showing my badge. My gun failed to impress anyone. I lost him."

Order began to drift into the gap on the sidewalk. "We found some stuff in the room," Metzger said. "Apparently we caught this guy coming back from the ice machine or something."

"Let's go check it out. Whoops, excuse me." He had turned and bumped into a man helping an elderly woman pick up her spilled packages. The man said nothing, but smiled absently. His steel-rimmed glasses kept sliding down his nose as he bent to lift up the bags on the sidewalk. He looked like a nice young man helping his mother. But he watched Tubbs and Metzger walk away until they rounded a corner and were out of sight.

Switek and Zito had arrived from the Flamingo, and Tubbs got the story on the shoot-out—or rather, the slaughter—from the guys who had witnessed it. SID was already at the Deseret, dusting the room and the Mercury for prints.

Grilling the manager turned up predictably disappointing results. The room had been occupied by one William Warren for five days. He took a lot of local phone calls. No numbers had been jotted down.

Tubbs saw Lou Rodriguez pull up outside, cutting through the police barricade. Uniformed officers tried to talk the spectators into doing something else this afternoon. Lou crawled forth from his unmarked sedan and squinted in the sunlight. As usual, half a mangled cigar stub was hanging from his lips, and his receding hairline was beaded with perspiration. Lou's characteristically rumpled suit arranged itself as he stood and straightened his spine. Lou's wardrobe, Tubbs knew, would always be a few degrees off true north. It allowed the head honcho of the vice squad to look expectedly harried when he reported to superiors. They would conclude Lou worked too hard and give him a raise. It was all a cunning strategy, thought Tubbs with a private smile. Crockett had vouched for him when he'd first hit the bricks in Miami, but it was Lou Rodriguez who took him on. In Crockett's words, Rodriguez was "one of the most righteous cops in the department."

People craving orders clustered around Rodriguez as he neared the room. Lou pointed and demanded—justifying a lot of existences in a short walk. "I want *everything* dusted and printed, and a report on my desk. No coffee breaks. Just do it. I want hair samples from the bathtub, prints from the car. I want to know whether he watched HBO or the Movie Channel last night. You got it? You find a matchbook cover, you run it through the lab. Scraps of paper, ditto—I don't care if it's toilet paper. Work the room, the parking lot, and out back. I don't care if you have to turn this whole motel—it's on my orders. So what are you looking at? Do it!" As he finished he came face-to-face with Tubbs. "About that little stakeout on Castronova, Tubbs—"

"Nobody figured he was a big enough fish to fry. He was a nothing middle-of-the-road dealer."

"He's not a nothing anymore, Tubbs. He's a triple homicide in broad daylight in the middle of a public place. Listen, I don't love these goons with the tags on their toes down at the morgue any more than you do . . . but *why* did they get smeared like that?"

"I wish I knew."

Switek rolled out of the room. "We got a briefcase," he announced proudly. "Looks like you cut him off from his hardware, Rico."

"Yeah?" said Tubbs. "What've you got?"

Switek led Tubbs and Rodriguez into the room. Lab workers dusted, and snapped photos. "Twenty grand in cash, couple of machine pistols . . ." He levered open the briefcase, which was sitting on the motel desk, with the end of his pen. ". . . and that."

Tubbs saw the tiny video screen, the keyboard, the roll of special paper for printout. "Personal computer. Fancy that." There were two cassettes slotted in the case's lid, beside spare clips for the pistols that were nestled barrel-to-butt in felt next to the computer.

"These okay for prints?" asked Tubbs of the nearest SID man, who nodded. He was ready to operate the portable device. "Plug me in, Switek; let's see what we got."

Lou nodded. He was intrigued. He puffed silently while Switek got on hands and knees to locate an outlet. He looked like someone's overweight uncle playing horsie. "You got juice," came a voice from beneath the desk.

Tubbs powered the little machine up and plugged in a cassette. When he tapped for a straight readout, he got a name:

BEAUDINE, BEAUREGARD - A174

"Beaudine's a coke dealer," said Lou immediately.

Tubbs tapped A174, and the green video screen began to roll up data: Beaudine's various addresses, aliases, make of cars, license numbers, phone numbers . . .

"Didn't Beaudine get himself shot to pieces at the beginning of the week down in Liberty City?" asked Switek.

"Yeah," said Rodriguez. "Is it all just on him?"

"Don't think so," said Tubbs, stopping the roll-up. "Let's see if there's another major index point." He touched some more keys. The screen cleared, and then a single line of green characters played out:

RUIZ, TRINIDAD A. - A777

"Another dealer," said Switek.

"Another *dead* dealer," said Rodriguez as Tubbs let the vital statistics on Ruiz play out. "Also blown away, also within the last five days—the time this guy has been living at the Deseret."

Tubbs stopped and keyed ahead. "Rudolfo Echevierra," he read. "God, if any of these guys were still alive, we'd have ourselves a little gold mine here."

"Carlos Tiendez," said Switek when the next name appeared. "All coke dealers. All scragged. Recently."

"Tubbs, can you call up a list of just the names?" asked Rodriguez.

"I think so." He tapped a few keys, then figured it out. "Here we go . . ." The simple list played out without the alphabetical name-reversal:

BEAUREGARD BEAUDINE
TRINIDAD A. RUIZ
RUDOLFO ECHEVIERRA
CARLOS TIENDEZ
ESTEBAN BARRENCIA
FELIX CASTRONOVA
LINUS OLIVER

"Oliver's not dead," cut in Rodriguez. "At least, not yet. Gina and Trudy are running surveillance on him."

"He's the only one on the list who's still with us," said Switek. "The only one who . . ."

He shut up because one more name appeared to finish off the list. Rodriguez went ash-white when he read it, and Tubbs' heart tried to jump out of his throat.

JAMES CROCKETT

"*Sonny* . . ." he whispered.

Rodriguez nailed him with a glare. "Where is Sonny right now, Tubbs . . . ?"

–4–

IN retrospect, Crockett would always remember the afternoon as a peculiar conjunction of fate. Thinking back to just a few hours earlier, he had certainly no reason to expect *anything* pleasant.

Starting with Janet Buckley, who'd been in a fighting mood. She wanted to negotiate Sonny's divorce from a "position of strength"—whatever *that* could mean—perhaps saving Sonny for *other* positions, once the case was history and Caroline gone. She was aggressive and well prepared. They had met without even a handshake and marched into battle, which awaited them at a table for two on the patio of the county courthouse.

Sonny did not miss the strategic significance of how no chairs had been provided for him and Janet. He realized instantly that this snide move had come straight out of the festering, plotting brain of Caroline's attorney, Alan Bisno.

As Janet and Sonny neared them, Caroline sipped coffee and nodded at Bisno. Her sharply pleated skirt showed off her legs. Sonny noticed with distaste just how often Bisno's bulging eyes dipped to appreciate them.

Caroline's eyes widened slightly—approvingly, perhaps?—when she saw Sonny's straight attire. She bit her lip. She looked as if she had just been awakened by bad news on the telephone and had not quite locked onto the real world yet.

But they didn't even have time to exchange perfunctory hellos. Bisno made the first move.

"Hi, Janet," he said, overly familiar, rising from his seat. "Mr. Crockett. Uh—listen, we've discussed this, and it's all really very simple. As custodial parent, my client is going to keep the boy no matter what case you might care to make. We got the American image of motherhood on our side . . ."

Janet stepped between Sonny and Bisno, getting right in the egg-eyed attorney's face. "You try it, Alan, and I'm prepared to ask for *and get* a four-county restraining order. You know I can do it. She'll never be able to take the kid north of Palm Beach!"

Bisno snorted. "Hah! Hardball? We'll bring up Mr. Crockett's . . . life-style. A vice cop who wades knee-deep in hookers, dope fiends, pimps, and scum all day, every day?" He laughed coarsely. "Doesn't even have a house. Doesn't even have an apartment? Hangs out with other lowlife cops who deal with the social dregs? He'll be lucky to see the boy once a year!"

Caroline stiffened at that. "I told you, Alan—visitation stays the way we discussed it."

Bisno waved her off. "Caroline, please let me handle this." He did not even look at her. She and Sonny didn't exist in this skirmish.

Sonny saw the word *help* in Caroline's eyes, and stopped shifting from foot to foot, cutting in before Bisno could resume his tirade. "Hold it. Time out." He got silence. "Caroline, can I speak to you?"

She rose from her seat without the slightest hesitation, but Bisno could not turn loose. "Caroline, there's no need for any extracurricular negotiations here."

She shot Bisno a glare that could vaporize lead shielding. "Don't push it, Alan," she warned softly, and Sonny felt a stab of pride. Caroline always had backbone.

She fell into step next to Sonny. They walked toward the courtyard fountain, closer than acquaintances but with enough space between them so they wouldn't be mistaken for lovers. Sonny drank in her image; he could not see enough of her at once. Caroline kept her eyes averted, then looked up, almost shyly. "Sonny . . . I had no idea he was going to be like this. I . . ."

"Don't say it," he said. "I caught the drift. Look, the only reason we got involved with these clowns in the first place was Billy. They act like they don't even know his name, like he's not even a human being. He's 'the boy.' 'The boy' this and 'the boy' that." Caroline nodded with a hint of a smile, as though only she and Sonny understood. "And Billy's a problem because you want to move back to Atlanta. You and I have *had* the arguments about my Vice gig. But Billy we never discussed; we automatically turned it over to the lawyers, like we sensed we'd do nothing but fight. But I can't stand to see what this does to you. I don't hate you. I don't even get mad at you..."

"That's one-way, I'm afraid," she said. "I always get mad at you." Her voice came out a little hoarse. "But never for long."

"Yeah." He savored a flash of memory, of brighter days. "Listen, if you think it's best to move back, and take Billy with you..." He shrugged. "No fight. No contest. Atlanta's an hour away by plane; I can come up damn near any time I feel like it. What the hell."

She allowed herself to open up a bit. "Sonny, I'm so turned around about all this. Now I feel that Billy does need to grow up around his father. It wouldn't be that much trouble for me to find another job down here."

He smiled. "You're in demand."

She nodded affirmatively. "You too."

Their gazes intersected, and to Sonny it was like being hit in the brain by a laser beam. When he had been stepping carefully through his last night with Gina Calabrese, even she had seen it. He tried to pretend he'd written his marriage off, while Gina had said it plainly: "You're still in love with Caroline." Now he felt a surge of desire for his wife so strong it rendered the world out of focus except for her face. She reached out and squeezed his hand.

With such a righteous lady, maybe he *could* work his life out.

Janet was trying to find something in the scenery to admire while Bisno hammered away. "Your client's a real Mister Rogers, y'know. I heard he lives on that boat with a twelve-foot-long alligator. Tch."

"See you in court, counselor," she replied acidly.

"Actually, I don't think you will," Caroline said as she and Sonny approached, considerably closer together. "And if you don't have any other cases, Alan, you won't be going to court, either."

Janet Buckley's mouth dropped open.

Sonny grinned his broad country-boy grin. "What the lady's trying to say is . . . you're both fired."

Bisno expressed no surprise beyond an annoyed sigh. "Okay, Caroline, let's stop this nonsense and get back into the . . ."

"Oh yeah, one more thing, scrub," Sonny interrupted. He stepped in eye-to-eye with Bisno. "You ever use that tone to Caroline again, and I'll wrap you around your endangered-species briefcase and drop-kick you into Biscayne Bay. You dig?"

Bisno gulped hard, but finally acquired the good sense to clamp a lid on his behavior.

"Sonny . . . ?" Janet was now at a loss as to how to proceed.

He patted her arm. "Call me and bill me for whatever I owe you, Janet. And tell Perry Mason there that Elvis is only ten feet long, not twelve, and he resents being spoken of in a disparaging fashion."

Caroline hid a laugh with her hand.

Leaving the two lawyers speechless, they walked off arm-in-arm, basking in the exhilaration of the changes they were working. They dumped their tension by laughing; it built until they were nearly crazy with relief—two battle-weary soldiers, veterans of the love wars, hanging onto each other for support.

"Welp," Sonny said in his best Gary Cooper voice, "our divorce was a bigger failure than our marriage." He held the driver's door of the Volvo for Caroline; and without suggesting any destination, she drove straight to their home.

They killed some spiked coffee. Caroline brewed, and Sonny dug out the remains of the brandy they'd gotten as a Christmas present two years before. So many pieces of their lives were entwined.

He rattled on for a while, and she let him. He talked of his work, but mostly about his growing friendship with Tubbs. She didn't ask him if he'd been seeing anyone, which let him gracefully avoid having to talk about Gina. He had the good sense not to ask her the same question.

Finally she said, "Billy won't be back from school until three or so."

Too quickly, he said, "You want me to go?"

She made a little mock gesture, as if to slap some brains into him. "The only place I want you to *go*, number eighty-eight, is with me." She grabbed his loosened tie and pulled him back toward the bedroom they had once shared—that was theirs again now.

* * *

"Like I said before we were interrupted, I was wondering if there wasn't some other reason." Caroline snuggled close to Sonny, one leg over his, her head on his shoulder.

"For?" He lay with his wife draped over him, absorbing her warmth. His hair was a riot.

"For us not going through with it today."

"Like?" He didn't want to break up the moment by talking.

She hesitated. "Like . . . like maybe I wasn't trying hard enough to make it work, you know, or trying hard enough to understand. Instead of griping."

"You always try hard."

She kissed each side of his mouth, then planted a more lingering one dead-center. "You ever have thoughts like that?"

"Nah." He shook his head. "Only two, three . . . hundred times, max. About as many times as I lay around my boat with my hand *this* far from the phone, hovering over it, an inch away from calling you in the dead of night. . . ."

"Unable to sleep? Torturing yourself? Having dreams about me, I hope?"

"Mm." The feel of her bare skin was fine, just missed and just familiar enough. "You ever have those kinds of thoughts?" he said.

"Nahh." She laughed softly and hugged him. They could not get any closer, but that did not stop them from trying. "Maybe this time, we'll . . ."

He put his finger over her lips, simply saying, "Yeah."

When the doorbell chimed, they both started, a little guiltily. He furrowed his brow. "Not Billy?"

"No. He doesn't come home by himself."

Sonny's expression grew sly. "A boyfriend. A lover?"

"Yeah, it's my two o'clock, wise guy. Sorry, but you'll have to go out the back way." She kicked off the bed sheet. Sonny's admiring gaze followed her nude form to the closet, where she plucked a bathrobe from a hook and tossed it around her with a lack of self-consciousness he found very stimulating.

She padded out barefoot. Sonny grabbed a pack of cigarettes from the nightstand, knocked one out, and lit it. There was a framed photo of the two of them, plus Billy when he was about three months old.

"Sonny?" The undertone of concern in her voice made something cold jump into Sonny's chest. He pulled on his pants and zippered up on his way down the hallway. The sight that greeted him was a little weird: Caroline in her robe, and Tubbs and Rodriguez on the front porch, looking way too grim. Not grim—downright *worried*.

"You two ever hear of giving a guy a break?"

Tubbs was mildly surprised to find Sonny here. He'd stopped by as a last resort, scared of what he might find. He'd driven out only when Caroline's phone had been busy for over two hours. Now he closed his eyes, exhaling in relief.

Only then did Sonny notice the squad cars lining the street. Three units, two officers each, plus his Corvette and Rodriguez' car.

Rodriguez said nothing. Tubbs withered a bit under Sonny's disapproving expression, then decided to jump into the thick of business. "Castronova got killed this morning just after we went off our stake-out."

"By whom?"

"We don't know. But it's strictly professional."

"Tubbs almost caught up with the shooter down on Bayshore," said Rodriguez around his soggy cigar. "He left behind a briefcase." He extracted from his pocket a curled slip of paper from the accountant-size printout sheet. "And in the briefcase was a little list."

Crockett scanned the paper. "Beaudine, Barrencia . . . upstanding citizens, all." To Caroline he added, "All midlist coke dealers."

"Eight names," said Tubbs before Sonny was finished. "And you're number eight."

"So? You guys wanna buy some coke?"

Rodriguez cut in. "It's a hit list, Crockett."

Sonny scanned the paper again. "You mean this is what all this . . . *support* is about?" He indicated the waiting squad cars. Neighbors were starting to peer through curtains. His stance relaxed. "Come on, fellas, I appreciate your concern, but I'd need about ten hands to count all the times my life's been threatened."

"There are eight names on the list, Crockett," Lou said with genuine worry. "The first six are in drawers in the morgue—all within the last five days."

The blood drained out of Caroline's face.

–5–

THE squad room whirled with calculated activity. Sonny was awed by the effort he had seemingly inspired. Amidst a hurricane of motion and purpose, even Switek and Zito manned the phones—squeezing information and updates. The objective was to get a thread on the mystery hit man.

Gina Calabrese racked the phone at her desk and settled her eyes on Crockett. Today she was all business; Sonny knew that privately she was as worried as anyone—more so, considering what they'd shared. "Okay," she said, checking off items on her pad, "what the portable computer files didn't have on the first names on the hit list, the DEA did have—all midlevel dealers, all starting to expand."

"Looks like somebody's bumping off the competition," Crockett said.

Tubbs leaned in. "What about SID?"

Gina waved the pad. *"Ninety-two* separate sets of prints and smudges in the hotel room. We're running the sets found inside the Mercury first. Should have feedback on those in a minute." A light on her desk phone flickered. "Hang on a second, guys." She picked it up.

Crockett could not remain still. He moved toward Rodriguez' office with Tubbs in tow. Lou was also on the horn as they walked in.

"I appreciate the rush, Jerry," Rodriguez said. "Yeah . . . I owe you one. I owe you *two*." He hung up. "Off the prints in the car, only one set rings a gong," he told them. There was very little hope or humor in his voice. "And of all places, Interpol."

"Has he got a name?" Crockett pressed.

"Nope. Sorry. No name at all. But the prints tie him into . . ." Lou tilted his glasses to read from the page before him. "1974—Allende's former ambassador to Mexico. 1976—a Turkish military attaché in Rio. 1977—two cultural attachés, one from Egypt, one from the Saudis, blown away in the Washington Hilton. 1981—Sandanista spokeswoman in Central Park. This is just the primary scan, but the list goes on like that for at least another page. Whoever this guy is, he's international. No loyalties. Plays either side of the political fence. They think he's Argentinian."

"That's all?" said Tubbs.

"One more statistic: he bats a thousand and has never taken a fall."

"Jesus." Sonny shook his head. "When you care enough, you only send the very best."

"Sonny?" Gina called, her hand cupped over the

phone. Something was on. "I've got Trudy; she's running surveillance on Linus Oliver. Turns out that yesterday he made several phone calls to someone named Rudolpho Mendez—the number matches up with the Deseret Motel."

"Run traces to the DEA, the Bureau, and ATF," said Rodriguez. "File an advisory to Interpol. Maybe we've got a label for this guy."

"Did Mendez set up any kind of a meet with Oliver?" said Sonny.

Gina shook her head no. "Not yet, at least—but they're supposed to negotiate for about fifty to a hundred kilos. It's just a matter of when Oliver makes the call."

"Stay on him. Tell Trudy not to lose him. Get some backup out to her."

Tommy Ray Zito boiled in, hyper as usual. "Got our confirm call from the safe house, lieutenant," he said to Rodriguez. "Caroline Crockett and the kid just arrived there in protective custody."

Gina was watching Crockett. At this news, he looked automatically to her. Assuming everybody got out of this mess alive, he knew he would have to tell Gina about his reconciliation with Caroline. Gina seemed to sense that events had suddenly raced up to a cliff edge.

He pushed it away from his mind, for later. "Who's at the safe house?" he said to everyone in general. Someone would perk up with a reply, he knew.

Zito ticked the men off on his fingers. "Monahan, Sweeney, Hebner, and Farris are there now."

Crockett's eyes flared at Lou. "You promised me six! What the hell is..."

"Jessup and Rosenthal are en route from downtown right now," Rodriguez said. "That's six. And with you safely stashed away up there with them, that's seven..."

"Oh no, Lou—I'm not running away from this. I'm going after Linus Oliver!" Crockett's fists were balled and his face was flushing. There was no way he was going to stand idle while the rest of the squad saved his ass.

With a deadly tone, like a pronouncement from a Supreme Court justice, Rodriquez said, "We've got it covered down here, Crockett. We don't need you."

"DEA's got an info sheet on Mendez," said Zito, "but it ain't much. No priors. No busts. No prints. No rap sheet. No photos. Connections in Bogotá. Residences in Miami, New York, Puerto Rico..."

"Got the Miami address?" said Crockett. If Mendez was the hitter, and he had a house in Miami, why had he been working out of a room at the Deseret?

"Yeah, but there's nobody there now."

"Local connections?"

"The top coke-stokers—the crème de la crème. He's a sometime drug-deal middleman."

"And a hitter? You sure you got the right guy?"

"He's the only guy we got so far, ace," said Zito huffily.

"How about a list of first-generation contacts. Just the repeaters?"

"I'll see." Zito trotted off to run the check, a can of Coke in one hand.

"Tubbs, let's go scoop this Oliver off the pavement before we have to make the coroner do it. Let's bring him in and see if he can make any sense out of this. Self-preservation is the great motivator." Sonny socketed a .45 automatic into his shoulder holster and checked the clip pockets on the opposite armpit of the web device. Then he reached for his coat. Rodriguez tapped him on the shoulder.

When he turned, he found Lou with no slack offered. "I told you, Crockett, I want you off the streets," he said—sternly enough to prove it was no joke, and loudly enough to stop the background natter of activity in the squad room.

Crockett faced off with his boss, steaming now. "Lou, I do my own work!"

Lou's eyes sparked. He was genuinely angry. "You wanna mess with me, Crockett? You are getting your butt into an unmarked car with bulletproof glass, and you are going into protective custody with your family. *That's* what you're doing, and I'm dragging you down there handcuffed if I have to!"

Crockett squelched. Gina, Tubbs, Zito—they were all watching, all concerned, and it twisted something sharp in his guts.

"I'm checking out the safe house myself," Rodriguez went on. "I've got two men down at your boat right now. We pick up your stuff, assign a babysitter to your dope-sniffing alligator, and we lock you in a cozy box where Mendez can't blow your heart out. Come on, Sonny, let's move it."

"Mendez' readout had Sonny's undercover address at the boat," said Tubbs. "Is it smart to go there at all?"

"He had to get close to Castronova," said Rodriguez. "And he won't be able to do that at the marina. Besides, he seems to be following the order of the hit list, and Linus Oliver is still walking and breathing."

"Breathing a lot easier than me," complained Crockett.

"Yeah, Lou, but Mendez knows by now that we've got his list."

"Come on, Lou," said Crockett, "the less time we spend here arguing, the sooner this whole thing is done."

Gina blew him a heartbroken little kiss, surreptitiously. Crockett acknowledged her as he and Rodriguez marched out.

One officer, Fields, wore duck pants and a work shirt. He sat in the stern of Crockett's sloop, the *St. Vitus Dance*, as far away from Elvis as he could get.

Fields' partner, Augustine, sat cross-legged atop the cabin. To his left was a high-powered automatic sniper's rifle. To his right was a box of DogNip—large, bone-shaped biscuit treats for man's best friend. Every so often—after he completed a sweep of the marina with his binoculars, looking for all the world like a nosy tourist on a rented boat—he dropped a biscuit into Elvis' waiting maw.

Elvis was leashed by his quarter-inch chromium mooring chain to the entrance hatchway to the galley. He had slithered down into the hold after his morning sunbath, and was miffed that his lunch of frozen perch was running late. He brightened up when Crockett appeared, and cut loose a bull-alligator roar of greeting that made Augustine recoil with second thoughts.

"Quite a critter you got here," Augustine said.

"Don't sweat Elvis, Mister A., he *likes* cops," said Crockett. He squatted to pat Elvis on the snout, and the creature rumbled. It was like purring, almost. "Just don't run out of DogNips. If you do, he likes crumb doughnuts just as well."

"Come on, Crockett!" Rodriguez barked impatiently. He gave Elvis a wide margin and said to Fields, "Give me those glasses. I want to have a look around here for myself."

Crockett hurriedly grabbed some things. His toilet kit, from the Flamingo stakeout that morning—a thousand years ago—was already in the car.

"Now, Augustine, there's plenty of perch in the hold. Whatever you do, don't let him near the digital clock by the bed. He'll eat it and get gas. Until you've experienced that, don't laugh. Whenever he eats the clock, it's a sign he's getting nervous and lonely. Or he's having a flashback. That happens sometimes on account of the flight bag full of LSD he ate—you remember that one. Or—I doubt this will happen, but it did once—he gets the urge to mate. Just keep him full of food. If he wants to crawl out and work on his tan, undo that section of the chain. And *whatever* you do, don't let that blue blanket outta his sight, or you'll have a reptile riot on your hands."

Augustine nodded like a man one drink beyond

his limit. Elvis grumbled, sensing Crockett was leaving. Parting was always such scaly sorrow. He crunched a DogNip into brown powder for solace.

Rodriguez scanned the perimeter with the field glasses. Several million dollars' worth of pleasure boats bobbed gently in the harbor. At the end of a man-made rock jetty, a lighthouse tower stood sentry. Most of the true lighthouses were no longer used these days, or bolted to plaques supplied by the National Lighthouse Society as quasi-monuments. Technology had made most of them obsolete. Some lone seeker hung onto the tower rail of the lighthouse, his windbreaker flapping madly in the ocean breeze. He was over two hundred yards away and was the only human being in sight.

"That's it, Lou. Let's boogie on outta here." Sonny was getting anxious to see Caroline and Billy, to simply reaffirm that they were okay.

Rodriguez handed the binoculars back to Fields and worked his way back toward the prow of the *St. Vitus Dance*. As he caught up with Sonny, out of pure chance he glanced back toward the lighthouse. It was a romantic relic—but it was the sort of romance that appealed even to Lou Rodriguez.

Lou saw the glint of light coming from the rail where the spectator had stood. Then the brass yachting lamp to the right of his head tore loose from its mount and spun past Augustine into the sea, with a huge, dented rip in one side.

"Crockett!" shouted Lou, diving. Sonny was out in the open. Lou hit him in a clumsy tackle and took him down.

Fields saw what was going down, leapt up,

snatched his own rifle from the deck, and sighted on the tower in time to see the windbreaker dart around to the opposite side—where the stairway undoubtedly was.

Augustine sighted through his own scope, but caught no movement.

Crockett tried to scuttle backward along the deck when he noticed that Lou, who was on top of him, was not moving or speaking. "Lou? *Lou . . . !*"

He rolled Rodriguez over. His eyes were glazing, and he was barely drawing shallow breaths. His pupils had dilated. There was a huge, pumping hole in his middle, and blood was running all over the deck. It was soaking into Sonny's pants.

"Suh . . . Sonny . . ." Lou's tongue had filled up his mouth; he couldn't quite believe he had caught a bullet.

"Augustine! Paramedic unit, now! Emergency! *Move it!*"

The pleasant-looking young man sheathed the massive rifle and slung it over his shoulder as he walked down the curving staircase inside the lighthouse tower. He stripped off his yellow-tinted shooter's glasses and replaced them with his steel-rims. He ran his fingers through his hair because the wind had mussed it.

The authorities had the list, he surmised—that's why the cop had panicked. Going after the cop because it was convenient, timewise, had proven to be a mistake. He was not completely certain that he had dropped the cop and not the bystander. He was no more squeamish about dropping noncontractees—"ducks," in his own argot—than he had been about coolly killing Felix Castronova's bodyguards. But it was extra service for free, and it offended his sense of symmetry and fair play.

The man with the schoolteacher face did not like squandering time on assignments. He had allotted himself a week to complete this multi-faceted one, but trying to speed things up by checking off the last name on the list, the eighth, *before* the seventh had proven to be an error. The original sequence had been best. He had weighed this opportunity, gambled, and perhaps lost. He had decided to try the lighthouse because, now that the police knew of the list, the cop would hide in protective custody and become hard to pick off.

"I didn't know the lighthouse was open for visitors," said a voice as he closed the ground-level door.

It was a woman of about fifty-five, in yachting pants and blinding white tennis shoes. She had a deep tan, a lot of sun wrinkles, a captain's cap, and about a hundred perfect white teeth.

The man with the steel-rims smiled pleasantly and held the door open so the woman could explore.

"Oh, thank you," she said. Then, more knowingly: "I had a hunch chivalry wasn't completely dead in this country!"

—6—

MARIA Rodriguez was a short, matronly woman, very Old World Spanish in appearance. Her handsome, strong face was puffed and distorted from weeping; her dark eyes wet. She, Crockett, and Tubbs could see Lou under an oxygen tent, through the private nurse's window that overlooked the intensive-care unit.

"Those the kids?" said Tubbs to Crockett under his breath, cocking a thumb back toward a couch in the waiting area.

"Yeah," Crockett said grimly. "Rebecca and Louis Junior. Sixteen and thirteen." Lou Jr. was wearing a Miami Dolphins sweatshirt, and Becky was snuffling.

A youngish doctor pushed through the swinging doors and muttered something privately to the nurse. Then he turned as the threesome converged on him.

"Mrs. Rodriguez?" He didn't seem interested in Crockett and Tubbs. "You should know, first of all, that your husband is in very critical condition. He'll be going back into surgery..." He consulted his wristwatch. "...in half an hour."

Rodriguez had been in the operating theater for over an hour the first time. The news that there was more to come caused Maria's tears to break the dam of control she had erected.

Crockett put his arm around her. She seemed very small. "Lou's tough, Maria. He'll pull through. He's not done cussing me out yet."

She smiled, nodded, moved off to tend her children. The doctor motioned Crockett to join him halfway down the sterile corridor; then, with a trace of anger, said, "I just want to know what the hell he was hit with, Officer Crockett. It left a hole big enough to throw a cat through. Looks like he was shot with a bazooka!"

Tubbs moved to join them. "Ballistics got the other slug from the boat. You're not gonna believe this, Sonny, but it was a fifty-caliber bullet."

The doctor looked to Crockett for an interpretation.

Sonny's mouth tightened. "Heavy caliber," he said. "The kind they used to use in the old Nitro Express buffalo rifles. Powerful."

"That I can see for myself," said the medico. "Massive hemorrhage, tissue trauma, thoracic trauma..."

"Downtown's already sent an interim substitute for Lou over to the Metro squad room," said Tubbs.

"Who?" said Sonny.

"Name's Swanson. Ring any bells?"

"Jesus! Bulldog Bailey Swanson, one of Lou's superiors. A Metro captain. Real heavyweight." He rubbed his face. "Okay. Let's go."

Tubbs' brow furrowed. "Go where?"

"To flush out Mendez." Crockett marched off down the hallway.

Tubbs had to trot to catch up. "Hey! What the hell you think you're doing? It's too hot out there!"

Crockett's shoulders were squared off, and he had that mean, pinched look to his face that Tubbs was growing to know as a signal for his stubborn determination. "You want me to sit around on some damned beach surrounded by guards while Rodriguez hangs by a thread down here and Mendez goes merrily after number seven? Not bloody likely. That bullet Lou took was meant for me, Tubbs!"

"Yeah, yeah, very noble, my man, I know all that—but look . . ." Tubbs had ahold of Crockett's arm, and when Sonny didn't turn his head, Tubbs spun him against the wall and shouted into his face. "You go out there, you're gonna wind up in traction right next to Rodriguez, if you're lucky. You're not listening to me, man!"

Crockett did not tense. He stared at Tubbs as though unsure of how to proceed.

"You can't go out there, you know?" Tubbs had Sonny's shirt fisted up in one hand. It was not until he looked down that he saw he had lifted Crockett six inches off the tiled floor. He eased up, embarrassed at such a passionate outburst. He could see reflected in Sonny's eyes the depth of the alliance they had forged so quickly.

Human beings, it seemed, were at their best when times and events were at their worst.

Tubbs looked down at the floor. "Nothing I can say is gonna stop you, right?"

Crockett shook his head; he was committed.

"Okay," said Tubbs. "Then let's go get this guy."

Crockett smacked him on the arm. No words were needed to convey his appreciation.

"Detective . . . uh, Crockett?"

Sonny's head jerked around. Already he was hypersensitive to strangers calling his name, in case one of those strangers might be holding a gun from Rudolpho Mendez on him.

It was a petite nurse. "Telephone for you."

"Stay cool, James," Sonny muttered to himself. "Yeah?"

"Sonny, this is Gina. You okay?"

"No. But what do you have?"

"Linus Oliver is on the move. He just got a call to set up a deal for twenty keys at some prearranged location. Wouldn't mention it on the phone, but Trudy's got a two-way tail set up on him."

"So follow him, already. We're not interested in busting him, Gina."

"The call was from Rudolpho Mendez. Oliver's meeting him in half an hour."

"Where!"

"Biscayne near Twenty-second. I thought you'd be interested."

"Gina, I love ya. Get another backup. I'm heading Oliver off before he gets a chance to get killed."

Tubbs had to chase Sonny out of the hospital.

* * *

"We're moving south on Second!" Tubbs said into the Corvette's radiophone as Sonny pushed the pedal to a cruising seventy per. "What's Oliver running?"

"White stretch limo," came Gina's voice. "Florida license MS DYNO. Third backup unit's just attached to him on Seventeenth Street."

"Give us three minutes to get there!"

"Make it two," said Sonny, eyes dead ahead. Their speedometer edged against the eighty mark as safe and conscientious drivers got the hell out of their way.

"Hold it, Tubbs," said Gina, long-distance. "We think Oliver has spotted the tail. His driver just pulled a highspeed U-turn over the divider!"

Crockett tucked the speeding Corvette neatly around a Metro bus. All the passengers stared. "Don't lose him," he said, beaming sympathetic magic Gina's way.

"We're stuck in traffic," reported Gina. "We're losing him . . ."

"Dammit!" Crockett slammed the dash. "Which way?"

"East on Nineteenth, toward Biscayne."

Crockett's anger turned to steely-eyed satisfaction. "Right into our waiting arms." He zigged past a lumbering Winnebago, zagged around a poking tourist in a Honda Civic, and cut the center lane for himself, barreling through an intersection a quarter-second after the light blinked to red.

"There," said Tubbs. Linus Oliver's white limo zipped past in the opposite lane.

"Hang on, Tubbs!" Crockett locked the brakes

and slid sidewise through the center divider. Oncoming traffic dovetailed and honked as the black car skidded backward, completing its 180-degree turn and aiming its nose to the front. Smoke billowed from the wheel wells as the car peeled out. The needle began to climb.

"I think he's made us," said Tubbs as the larger vehicle began to pick up speed. Its pilot was good; he dodged the elephantine car around a hard, red-light corner. Pedestrians screamed and leapt for cover. Crockett steered the Corvette through the swath Oliver had cut, and gained on him. It was no contest. The limo clipped the second turn and rode up on the pavement, clearing away a mailbox, a pay phone, and two vending machines for the sex tabloids before thwacking nose-first into a concrete street-lamp pole. Two tires were riding the gutter; two were up on the sidewalk.

As Crockett and Tubbs emerged from the Corvette, weapons drawn, the van containing Trudy and Gina pulled up on the opposite side of the street. The two female vice cops, both with their guns out, scampered across the street. Gina swore loudly at the traffic that refused to let them pass. Crockett admired her nerve.

Linus Oliver hauled his bulk from the rear of the limousine. Oliver's sheet listed him as the owner of a nightclub called What's Your Sign. He was big, broad, and black, duded up in a black suit, black pants, and a black turtleneck, with a gold sunburst medallion hanging on a thick chain. As Linus unhorsed himself, two of his enormous African bodyguards off-loaded from the front seats of the limo. Linus was all surprise and phony smiles.

"So where do you think you're going?" asked Tubbs, aiming at Linus' head.

Linus grinned, his huge cheeks swelling up. "To the car wash. Guess I need to go to the body shop first, now."

Crockett, apparently, had dealt with Linus before—or maybe it was just that coke dealers acted slaphappy all the time. Either that, or they were paranoid gunslingers like Barrencia, or slimeballs like Castronova. "You always take your two babysitters along?"

Linus made a face. "Car wash is in a bad neighborhood." He peeled back his cuff and checked his twelve-thousand-dollar Rolex. "My, my—lookee here how time flies! I'm runnin' late for a business appointment, gents. *Ciao . . .*"

Tubbs interposed himself between Linus and the limo. The guards bristled, but Tubbs ignored them. "You're running late for *life*, slick. You read the papers? You can read, can't you? Dealers just like you have been dropping like flies in a vacuum!"

Linus, from experience, played it fat, happy, and dumb. "Dealer? Watcha mean—like a car dealer?"

Crockett had had enough. "Where'd he stash the suitcase, Trudy?"

Trudy pointed with her gun barrel. "The trunk."

Linus' mouth dropped into an O of surprise. "You guys been runnin' surveillance on me?"

Tubbs elbowed past one of the bodyguards, reached in to the dashboard, and popped the trunk.

"Hey! Hey!" Linus protested, jittery now. "You dudes is infringin' on my Constitution!"

Crockett hauled out a large silver case. "Keys, please, Linus."

Linus folded his thick arms, pouting. "Forget it, Jack. Got no right to open that suitcase!"

Crockett, fed up, stuck the muzzle of his .45 against the suitcase latch and blew it off with one round. Its pieces tinkled on the sidewalk. He dropped the lid back. Packed inside were neat packets of cocaine and stacks of banded century notes. It was about a fifty-fifty split between the blow and the hundred-dollar bills. Crockett gave Linus his school principal expression. "Mm-mm-mm . . ."

Linus knew that a vice cop could get away with opening the case on probable cause, so he didn't pursue it. Instead, he assumed a shocked expression regarding the suitcase's contents. "Lookee here at that! Where'd all that come from?"

"Pray tell! The Tooth Fairy?" Crockett slammed the case shut. "You oughta get out of the slam sometime in the twenty-first century, Linus, old pal."

Tubbs, standing next to Linus, assumed a magnanimous air. "Say, Sonny—why don't we just let the brother go?"

Linus looked suspiciously at him. Some sort of scam was going down.

"That's not a bad idea, Ricardo. It'd save the taxpayers room service and linen bills. Relieve the overcrowding in our correctional institutions. Hit the bricks, Linus."

Linus was not about to question this. He waved his bulldogs back into the limo and saluted Tubbs and Crockett. Of the dope, he said, "Finders keepers," and turned his back on it. Tubbs stopped him.

"No, no, amigo. You keep it. We don't want it," said Tubbs, patting the big dealer on the back. To Crockett he added, "Eight to five Linus is history by . . . noon tomorrow. Half of whatever cash is in the suitcase."

"I'll take those odds," Crockett said. "I say he'll be breathing until midnight at least."

Linus, all too eager to hit the bricks, now froze. "Yo! Whoa! What's this crap you're talkin'?"

"Don't you understand, Mister GQ man?" said Tubbs. "You are *numero seven* on Rudolpho Mendez' hit list. You think he called to match nickel-and-dime stuff like that suitcase? He called you up so he could off you."

"First six guys on Mendez' little list are already on slabs," said Crockett. "You know Esteban Barrencia? Felix Castronova? Both hit this morning."

Linus suddenly became very sensitive to the idea that they were all public as they stood there. "Uh . . . let's get outta the open, man . . ."

"No way. I like the sunshine, fresh air, vitamin C! Now, if you want to take a little hike with us, well . . ." He shrugged.

Linus fell into step between Tubbs and Crockett. They walked half a block in silence. "Tell me about the suitcase," said Sonny.

Conscious that he might be able to talk himself out of taking a courtroom fall for the dope, Linus said, "I was just holding it, y'know, for this guy. It wasn't mine . . ."

"Holding it, or holding out on him?" Linus acted

grumpy, offering no response. "Earth to Linus? Come in Linus . . . ?"

"Why would Mendez want to bump you off, Linus?" asked Tubbs. "An upstanding citizen like you? Why those other dealers?"

"Cause he don't like independent competition," said Linus. "No freelancers." He shoved his hands deep in his pockets.

"Mendez doesn't want competition? Mendez isn't that deeply into dope."

"Not Mendez. The Colombian. Mendez used to work for the Colombian."

Crockett and Tubbs stopped dead. Linus walked three paces ahead before he realized he was alone. "You mean Francisco Calderone?" said Tubbs, meeting Crockett's gaze.

"Yeah—that's the dude. Mendez used to be his middleman."

"How long?" said Crockett.

Linus pondered. "Two months. Or three. The Colombian's old right arm got blowed away by the cops."

"Trini de Soto." Crockett knew the name because he and Tubbs were the cops that had killed de Soto—who had also been a sometime hitter for Calderone.

"That's right," said Linus. "I figured Mendez had gone solo, since Calderone got run out of the country."

"They're still good pals," said Crockett. "Calderone never liked anybody aceing him out." Crockett had lost his former partner in a car-bomb explosion designed for one such dealer who had broken away from Calderone's fold—a young brain-damaged case named Corky Fowler.

Tubbs said nothing. He had come down to Miami after Calderone ordered the death of his brother, Rafael Tubbs. At last, he said, "Calderone has a very long reach . . . and a very strong hand."

"No mistake, Linus, Mendez would have had a bullet waiting for you at Bayshore Park after he collected Calderone's goodies back. You got a phone number for Mendez?"

"Yeah—his mobile phone."

They came back around to the limo where Gina and Trudy awaited them. "Call him," Crockett commanded Linus. "Tell him the deal's still on."

Playing along, Linus seated himself in the plush cabin and punched buttons on the phone set into the armrest. "Hello? Yo, Carlos, my man! Say, I gotta apologize to you for this afternoon, man. I got tied up with some last-minute business. You know how it is . . ."

Tubbs motioned for Linus to cover the mouthpiece. "Make it someplace isolated. Airport parking lot C. Third level."

Linus nodded. "Tonight is great. Yeah. You know the airport . . . ? What? My club? No, man—club's jammed up with too many people, loud music, crowded . . ." He was overridden. "Yeah, okay, upstairs. Slide on by, man. Yeah . . . solid." He hung up with a sour expression. "Mendez likes crowds, it seems." Then he brightened. "It's time for me to check out, y'all. You dudes take over." He started to close his door.

Tubbs blocked it with his foot. "Guess again."

Linus frowned in momentary incomprehension, then realized, when he saw their faces, what the vice cops were reaching for. "Ho, no! No freakin' way, Jack! If you thinking what I think you be thinking, ain't no way I'm gonna walk in there and get my face shot off! You lookin' at a conscientious objection! No, man, look, it's simple: the dude walks in the door, you grab him. Easy!" He was sweating buckets now.

"Small problem, me bucko," said Crockett. "We don't know what he looks like. You've got to spot him for us. And if you don't, you got your choice of a permanent bunk in the nearest concrete Hilton—or a refrigerator-size hole in the ground." He enjoyed watching Linus squirm.

It was too much for Linus. His world had turned to garbage in the space of ten minutes. "I shoulda gone on to podiatry school; I just knew I shoulda done that."

Grandly, Tubbs said, "But then you wouldn't rate the Trudy-Gina Escort Service." To the ladies he turned and presented Linus: "Have I got a man for you!"

"Oh yeah?" said Trudy dourly. She crossed the street to their van and pulled it over.

Tubbs waved. "Stick with him, ladies!"

Linus had succumbed to the inevitable. Deflated, he said, "Yeah, stick with me, ladies . . ."

Gina held the sliding panel door for him. "You stick yourself in your place, baby-cakes. Step right in." Linus hurried inside and she slammed the door.

Crockett returned from having told the bodyguards to run the limousine along home. They watched as Trudy and Gina tooled Linus away for safekeeping. The Corvette was still curbed where they had left it.

"You stay here," said Tubbs. "I'll bring up the car."

Crockett frowned. "Nice try, Tubbs. But I think I can walk half a block without getting killed." But his eyes darted nervously to the left and right all the same. He was shaken, but maintaining. Tension like this would ultimately snap him like a guitar string.

Tubbs finally voiced it. "Calderone. He's behind all this, Sonny. Bumping off competition that grabbed the territory he left open when he split the country. Staging a comeback. Smoothing over the past. And nailing the cop that busted him."

"Why me and not you?"

"It was easy for somebody with Calderone's resources to find out that you were the Miami heat. Nobody down here knew my name. Far as he was concerned, I was just a no-name cop who got the drop on him before *you* arrested him."

"Calderone would have the clout and the connections to hire an international hit man. God knows how good this guy is, Tubbs—I just got lucky out at the boat, and look what happened to Lou!"

"You cost Calderone two million dollars, Sonny. He jumped bail."

"I guess that's reason enough. I don't know anybody who's worth that much to me." Then he forced a grin. "Except you, Caroline, Billy, Gina, Elvis—"

A hand clamped itself on Crockett's shoulder from behind and a voice said, "Hey!"

Crockett spun instantly and stuck the muzzle of his already cocked .45 right in the center of the stranger's forehead. It was an elderly man whose eyes went wide with fear. His hand, which held a crumpled pack of Lucky Strikes, trembled uncontrollably.

"Uh . . . you dropped these," the old gent said in a quavering voice. Suddenly, guiltily, Crockett became aware of the people milling around—citizens on their shopping rounds who had no idea who he was and what he did. He saw a pair of little girls no more than six years old caper past, scarfing down sno-cones. A construction worker wearing a hard hat started to intercede, bravely oblivious to the threat of the gun.

"Hey, you son of a . . ."

Tubbs blocked him. "Police," he said, flashing his badge. "A little mistake, that's all."

"Sorry," Sonny said in a choked voice, with the crazy impulse to add *I thought you were somebody else*—the sort of line one used to pick up strange women. He stowed his piece and gingerly accepted his cigarettes back.

The tide of workers and shoppers flowed back around them. "Hey man," said Tubbs, "you all right?"

Disgusted, Sonny said yeah, he was fine. Together they double-timed back to the car. "A little jumpy, though."

"Yeah, I'd say so!"

"That was one lucky citizen back there—not to

mention me!" He was forcing his better nature to the surface.

They climbed into the car and tooled away. The man wearing the steel-rimmed glasses, who had watched the whole incident, stood near a bus-stop bench eating a cherry sno-cone. The two little girls walked right past him, one of them dropping a soggy twist of napkin on the sidewalk. He stopped them and demonstrated that using the litter basket was preferable. Then he smiled. They giggled at him in unison and complied. Their mother, who had to run to keep up with them in the afternoon foot traffic, saw what had transpired. She bestowed a dazzling smile on the stranger before herding her daughters off.

He liked to think of himself as a small force for good manners in the world.

—7—

THE foaming surf of the Atlantic pounded into the cove and foamed over the rocks, retreating, marshaling for its relentless, eon-long combat with the shore. It eroded the land over millions of years. It never stopped. Never.

Crockett was beginning to view his diaphanous opponent, whom he had never even seen, the way he viewed the ocean—as an unopposable force of nature. That was wrong, and deadly. The hit man was a human being—even as Calderone. Both of them could be stopped.

If Crockett himself didn't get terminated first.

Gulls wheeled on the sea thermals overhead. The breakers crashed in and soaked the sand. Billy, shirtless, bouncing about in his too-big Bermudas, attacked the damp sand with his little red shovel, foraging for subsurface life-forms. Caroline's honey-colored hair was buffeted by the offshore breeze. She wore bikini bottoms and one of Sonny's old work shirts, and Sonny modestly thought she was gorgeous. He wrapped an arm around her shoulders and hugged her close as they walked. It seemed to be a perfectly idyllic setting.

Except for the armed guards and the machine guns.

Crockett knew most of the men standing watch over the safe house, which was located an hour out of Miami on private beachfront property. The location was neither written on paper nor recorded in any computer record. It was classified. The guards were checked out on military-customized American 180's, the weapon the CIA favored for guarding the President. The windows in the safe house were made of bulletproof glass with a 10-percent diffraction—with anything seen through the window actually five inches to the left of where it appeared to be. Every precaution had been taken.

"Sonny," Caroline said, "I've never been this scared before."

"It's the last thing you and Billy deserve." He had explained to her why Calderone needed to eliminate him, thus putting everyone in danger. The hitter was not afraid to shoot through another person—and chances couldn't be taken, not with other people like Caroline or Billy. "Don't worry, darlin'—nothing's going to happen to us."

She looked past him, doubtfully. "Then promise me you'll stay here." She registered his expression. "Sorry. I'm trying to stay cool, you know. But I'm losing it."

He stopped and wrapped her up in his arms. "No, you're *not,*" he said into her hair. "I can't stay. Rodriguez is in the hospital; the people I work with have got their butts way out on the line for me."

She knew all this. And held him in silence.

"Dad!"

"Hey, sport—what'd you dig up?"

Billy poked at something with his finger, then jerked his hand back, unsure. "It's a crab!"

"Oh, a little hermit crab . . ." He hunkered down next to his son. The kid was getting so big so fast. "Now, listen to me, kiddo. I need you to do me a favor. I want you to promise me you'll take care of your mom."

His face screwed up into a very important expression. Billy quickly said okay.

"Great. Now give me a hug."

Billy hugged his dad; Crockett lifted him off the ground. "Whoa—you're getting too big to pick up!"

"We goin' swimming now?"

Crockett's face darkened. "No, son, I'm sorry. We'll go swimming tomorrow, okay?"

Billy looked at him in the same doubtful way Caroline had. Caroline had a hard time watching. Crockett could see the fear living in her face, sabotaging her strength. In microcosm this was a replay of their whole marriage. He bent over, and Billy untwined his skinny arms from around his father's neck. There was nothing left to say. He turned and walked toward where Monahan waited for him with the escort car.

"Wave bye-bye," Caroline said to Billy, who complied.

Sonny waved, then left his family in the care of the police.

The outpouring blast of music rocked Tubbs back on his Gucci heels. What's Your Sign was rocking and rolling this night, with a near-capacity crowd corraling around the bar and bumping on the dance floor. A disco light setup rendered the whole scene in neon tones—a swarming, rolling seascape of expensive clothing and strategically exposed flesh.

Tubbs bowed grandly, allowing Trudy Joplin to precede him. She had dropped a ghostly and revealing gown of pale blue silk over her body, and it clung in just the right places. It was gathered up loosely at one shoulder and attracted a lot of attention.

Gina was no less spectacularly decked out, in black, low-cut satin. She acted out her part as Linus Oliver's lady of the evening. Following her through the front door was Linus, perspiring and looking uptight.

Giorgio, Linus' natty, tuxedoed doorman, hurried up to greet them. "I'm dynamite, Giorgio. Uh, listen, why don't you put us way in the *back*, tonight . . . ?"

Tubbs collared Giorgio and said, "His usual table." Giorgio looked uncertainly to Linus, who nodded in confirmation. Then he led them inside.

A would-be *Dance Fever* superstar swung his flapper girl friend over his head. Her long dancer's legs scissored through the air.

On their circuitous route back to Mr. Oliver's table, Tubbs passed a waiter with slicked-back hair who was leaning over the bar and yelling at the bartender: ". . . and a couple of Paulis! Hurry up, I got thirsty boogie-people waitin' on me out here!"

The waiter was Zito, in a leather apron, with rolled-up sleeves. The barman, Switek, rounded Zito's order together on a tray. "How's it going out there?"

"Not too shabby," Zito said. "Made twenty-five bucks in tips so far, and got two phone numbers."

"Gimme a break," Switek growled back. "And *smile!*"

On his way back across the floor, Zito stopped to trade a sentence or two with one of the dancers—another cop. The costume she was hanging out of barely left room to conceal anything, let alone a gun; but Zito knew she packed a most artfully hidden one, in a place not to be bragged about on the six o'clock news.

Crockett surveyed the scene from the roped-off balcony level, leaning with his arms spread out on the rail, his .45 cinched beneath his armpit. Next to him, an extremely intense SWAT team sniper named Bob crouched. He had his ball cap on backward, like a goofy oddball in some teen beach movie, and he cracked his gum as he talked.

"Willya for godsake sit on your hands, Crockett?" he said, exasperated. "We got it covered, man."

"They look like sitting ducks down there."

"This is a piece of cake, man. I mean, look at the vantage we got ourselves up here. Not to worry. Once, I had to pick off a dude in a shopping-mall bank robbery. He had a lady hostage in a strangle-hold with a forty-four jammed in her ear. I just held my breath and squeezed the old trig. Bingo! Right in the forehead. My slug was heavy enough to blow him away before the muscles of his trigger finger could contract."

"Charming." His hands vised the rail. *He* was safe up here, thinking that maybe Bob the SWAT sniper and Mendez could trade shoptalk over a couple of brews.

Bob grinned. "I just do my job."

Linus fidgeted behind his appointed table. Tubbs was a dapper picture of cool. "Gina—time?"

She glanced at a diamond-encrusted watch. "Six till ten."

Linus' eyes went wide with alarm. "The dude in the red shirt—over there!"

Tubbs, instantly alert, fixed on the guy.

Linus' expression sagged. "No. That ain't him." After mopping his brow, he added, "I ain't cut out for police work."

Zito arrived with a tray of champagne for them. Tubbs glanced at the bottle of Piper-Heidsieck. "Gee, Linus," he said as Zito popped and poured, "this is classier than I'd expect from you."

"It may be my last toast," Linus said glumly. "What did you expect?"

"Oh—Maison Blanc, three bottle for five dollars." As Linus frowned, the girls laughed.

When they had killed a round, Tubbs asked for another time hack.

"Hell, it's two after, people. The dude ain't gonna show," beefed Linus. "Why don't we all just cruise on out of here, hm?"

Gina was saying that Zito as a waiter looked like

Jerry Lewis in *The Errand Boy* when Zito spot-checked them.

Concern crept into Tubbs' voice. "It's getting way too crowded in here, Zito."

"You tell me! It's like a sardine can out here, fulla live sardines!"

Gina noticed, and turned to Trudy. "You want to dance—and circulate?"

"I thought you'd never ask, sugar."

"Remember," Tubbs warned as they rose to move off, "he could look like anyone. Might even be in disguise. Watch for any kind of signal from Linus."

They blended into the bumping, grinding throng of dancers, moving methodically, recording faces in their minds and being professionally unobtrusive.

Tubbs poked the ear-set in and keyed the volume on his walkie-talkie unit. "Peterson, we can no longer see the front door," he called. That brought another unsettled look from Linus.

"I wonder how come it is I don't have no faith in law enforcement," he said, pouring himself another glass.

Face after face strobed past in the crowd. Any of them might be the hitter. Gina got hip-bumped, hard, and arrested her imminent fall by grabbing onto the bar, muttering, "One more person steps on my foot, I'm gonna start shooting."

"How about a ginger ale?" called Switek.

"You're on." She massaged her bare toes.

Trudy tried to wend her way back toward Gina through the crush of party animals, but suddenly her path was blocked by a muscle-bound black dude bulging mightily out of a tight Superman glitter

T-shirt. Even over the deafening barrage of funk, his booming voice was quite clear. "Hey, let's *dance*, pretty young thang!"

She smiled civilly. "Sorry. All danced out."

He grabbed her arm in a vise grip, and she saw that he was lit to the rafters. "Ho—not yet you ain't!" He clamped his other hand around her backside and pulled her to him. Zito appeared.

"Hey man—cool out!"

"Kiss off, white bread!" Superman snarled.

Gina elbowed toward them and slapped the black paw away from the front of Trudy's gown. "The lady doesn't want to dance!" she declared. She then found herself grabbed rather rudely from behind by Superman's old army buddy, Superman Two, who cackled, *"Saaay,* you're a feisty li'l old thang, mama!"

They were backed up against a table housing a huge Samoan wrestler-type wearing a loud floral-print shirt and a crisp white jacket. Gina grabbed a champagne bottle from his table and broke it over Superman Two's head. "No violence, now," she warned. The dude staggered backward with bubbly fizzing in his Afro.

Superman then made a swinging grab for Gina. Trudy blocked him and Zito punched him in the nose. He wheeled back and upended the top-heavy cocktail table, drinks aplenty, all over the enormous Samoan. Then Superman Two leapt on Zito from behind, and the pocket riot began to blossom like a typhoon in the middle of an ocean.

"Outta my face, busboy!" shrieked Two, punching and flailing. Zito spun and sank a foot into the man's gut, shutting him up. Courtesy of the Samoan, Superman flew—over their heads and into the bar rail. By then, drunken strangers were gleefully joining in the free-for-all.

Linus jerked and grabbed Tubbs' arm, too tight. "I see him—right there, yellow shirt!"

Tubbs hit the walkie-talkie. "He's inside. Yellow shirt, near the front door."

"Dammit," spat Crockett as he watched the fight spread out below him. "This is just what we need!"

"Peterson!" yelled Bob into his own radio. "Block off the door! Stop the people from piling in!"

Three SWAT men appeared from nowhere and formed a wedge in front of the door that no one was crazy enough to challenge. Then they began to work their way in, cutting through the crowd like a weed eater.

Giorgio, the maître d', and a burly What's Your Sign bouncer had each grabbed a tree-limb-like forearm of the angry Samoan, who lifted them both into the air like light barbells. The deejay in the booth, grooving on the fight, cranked up the ZZ Top to background it. Tubbs could only catch a here-and-there flash of the suspect's yellow shirt.

Crockett could see the hitter just fine. "To hell with this crap!" he said, and burst past Bob the sniper to run down the stairs and edge around to the bar. Once there, he jumped on top and ran the length of the polished hardwood, catching Yellow Shirt's neck in a twisting, flying tackle worthy of his semipro football days. Number 88 lived. And the man in the yellow shirt collided hard with the floor as, all around him, guns appeared and were pointed.

When Trudy, Gina, Zito, and the others whipped out their iron, the bar fight calmed from a boil to a simmer with lightning speed. Eighteen weapons, including Bob the sniper's, were trained in the suspect's direction. Last of all, Crockett wrestled the man right-side-up and jumped on top of him, tearing his .45 loose and planting the bore right between the mustachioed man's brown eyes.

"You blink . . . cough . . . pass gas . . . and you're very dead," said Crockett with supreme deadliness. The ring of cops moved in closer for a look at the dreaded and feared Argentinian hit man.

The expression on the downed man's face was more one of surprise at his reception committee than anything else. His gaze sought Linus Oliver, who had tried to slip away but had been apprehended by Gina and Trudy, who led him, hammerlocked, to the bar.

"That Mendez?" said Gina. Linus nodded, and she released him. Busting Linus the coke dealer was a deal for another day.

Right-handing his automatic, Crockett reached into Mendez' shirt pocket and extracted the broken halves of a pair of thick, black plastic sunglasses.

"You busted my shades," Mendez said into the gun barrel.

The tension broke. Mendez was collected and everyone relaxed.

Nobody, not even Linus Oliver, knew that while

the man they had busted was in fact Rudolpho Mendez, he had never been to Argentina, had *never* had a pleasant face, and had never needed glasses in his life.

–8–

"BREATHING a bit easier now?" Tubbs ribbed Sonny, outside What's Your Sign.

"Absolutely. I even feel like kissing Linus Oliver."

"Too late. He's already boogied for home."

Crockett started laughing, part exhaustion, part nervous tension. "Yeah, he's had a pretty rough day." Tubbs joined him. Crockett wiped his eyes, looked down the barren and forbidding street lit up by nighttime reds and greens. "I'm going to the safe house. I want to get Caroline and Billy out of there. I want to take my family home."

Tubbs watched as Monahan pulled the unmarked cruiser to the curb. "I'll grill Mendez downtown. I'll take your car down there. You meet me in a couple of hours; I'll wait up for you. I'm sure you'd like to ask him a few things."

"About Calderone." Crockett nodded. "You bet

your life." He moved for the cruiser, then turned back. "Thanks, buddy. You put yourself on the line for me."

Though Tubbs knew this sort of admission was a rarity for Crockett, he shrugged it off. "Hell—I help out all my friends on the hit list."

He watched as Crockett's taillights dwindled away. At the Metro station, he let Mendez sweat it out alone in one of the interrogation booths while he nabbed a cup of coffee. Calderone was still screwing up their lives, long-distance. Calderone had to be erased for good.

The first thing Mendez said when Tubbs entered the cork-paneled room was, "My attorney isn't here, man. You know the rules." Mendez was very collected now. He seemed to have realized what had happened—and based his cool on data Tubbs and the others knew nothing about.

"We got your little computer, Mendez, so let's not talk lawyers just yet," said Tubbs. "They're a waste of good bread. We haven't decided yet whether you were shot trying to escape."

Mendez smiled pleasantly and folded his arms.

"Esteban Barrencia," Tubbs read from the list. "Felix Castronova. Et cetera. A tally of six murders you pulled in a hair over five days."

Mendez started laughing, unable to contain himself.

"I want to know where Francisco Calderone is. In this country? In the Caribbean? Out of Florida, in the U.S. at all? Where?"

Mendez was shaking his head, as if at an idiot.

Switek looked to Tubbs from his end of the interrogation table. *So what do we do now?*

"Calderone who?" Mendez repeated for the fifth time.

"The state is going to exterminate you, scuzzbag. They'll crank up the juice just for you, and you'll fry."

"No, I won't," countered Mendez, "not on the word of a clearly insane cop. I didn't kill nobody. And I don't know where you got the crazy idea I did. *Tu sabes?*"

"Where is Francisco Calderone? You know we've got all week, Mendez, and we get dinner breaks."

Utterly composed, Mendez had been through this process before; he hung onto his party line. "Calderone who?"

Trudy stuck her head through the door. "Tubbs—pick up line four, right now." She was still wearing the gown that was going to make sleeping impossible for Ricardo Tubbs, no matter *how* rough his day had been.

He stepped out and held the phone to his ear. Gina sat on the nearby desk, watching Switek and Mendez through the one-way glass. She saw the way Tubbs' face drained even in the subdued blue light of the observation room.

Slowly, he racked the phone. "That was Ballinger, from Homicide. Linus Oliver just got blown to pieces in front of his apartment building—just like Castronova. Automatic weapons. Trashed the whole limo, the bodyguards, and Linus. The guns were left at the scene. Woman says *maybe* it was a dude wearing a gray racing jacket who held the door for her . . . but nobody is sure about anything."

Gina was staring at him, scared. Then she looked back at the man they'd held in custody for the last hour and forty minutes.

"Gina, we've got the wrong guy. The hitter is still out there."

"Oh my God," she said, "Sonny . . ."

She grabbed for the nearest phone while Tubbs raced back into the interrogation room.

The door to the safe house was opened by a sentry clad in body armor and toting an M16. Crockett saw Caroline standing halfway down the entry hall, a hopeful but cautious look on her face. She had not slept.

"It's over," he said quietly; and just as quietly, she came to him.

Billy wandered out, rubbing his eyes, and saw his mom and dad in a tight embrace, framed by the light spilling through the doorway. His logical response was to join up, trying to make his smaller arms hug both of them at the same time. If he hadn't been protecting his mom, he thought, his dad would not look so happy.

For that moment they were physically and spiritually united, and Sonny noticed that even the guards seemed to breathe easier.

They took Caroline's Volvo back to the house, *their* home. There were many things to discuss, but both Caroline and Billy nodded off in their seats during the return trip. Crockett spent most of the drive contemplating his own green reflection in the windshield, wondering how it would play when they were all rested, awake, and opinionated. His odds weren't very good, but they weren't nonexistent, either.

After he had parked in the driveway, he rousted everybody from slumber. The house was dark and lifeless; not even the porch light was on. He bundled Billy together in his A-Team sleeping bag, mashed Caroline against him under one arm—she was still warmly drowsy, and her steps wandered—and steered the group toward the front door.

He fiddled with the car's key ring. "God, Caroline, you have ninety keys on this thing! Which . . . ?"

"Some detective," she mumbled, grabbing the ring and deftly opening the bolts. "Billy, make sure you aren't coated with sand before you come in."

She took Billy while Crockett slung her garment bag over one shoulder. The first order of business was to call Tubbs. He dumped the bag on the sofa and hit the vestibule light. It threw most of the living room into soft relief. He located the phone on the coffee table and, out of habit, picked it up to crook it against his waist while he punched the Touch-Tone buttons.

The phone cord was disconnected.

No one had been in the house, and the phone was disconnected.

"Crockett's phone is ringing," said Gina, "but nobody's there."

Tubbs slammed through into the interrogation cubicle, his eyes hot and fierce. "Where is he?" he snapped at Mendez. "Where's the hitter?"

Mendez just sneered, getting ready to say *Calderone who?* again.

Tubbs shot across the room, grabbing Mendez' throat in one hand and bulldogging him into the opposite wall. Mendez skull dented the soundproofing. "The hitter! Where is he?"

A look of fear dashed across Mendez' face—Tubbs had wanted to shatter the dude's cool exterior—but was quickly replaced by calm, like something alive and squirming being sucked into a quicksand pit. "I ain't gonna tell you nothing, man," he hissed. "Zip. Go rot and die."

Tubbs cocked his fist to smash Mendez' smug expression into goulash, but his swing was arrested by Switek. "This sleazeball isn't the shooter," said Tubbs, "but he knows who is—and the shooter is still out there."

It dawned on Switek. "Goin' after number eight?"

Tubbs' expression told him all he needed to know. Tubbs pushed off, forgetting Mendez. "Come on, Switek, we gotta hit it, now! It may already be too late!"

They dashed out and vaulted into the Corvette, Tubbs gunning the engine and peeling out of the lot with much smoke and noise. Switek grabbed the mobile phone and tried Crockett's house again. "Still nothing." He dialed Captain Bailey Swanson and found that Crockett and his family had left the safe house nearly an hour ago. "They should be home by now," he said.

"Maybe they already are," Tubbs said ominously.

Switek hung on while Tubbs slid through a red light and jammed down the thoroughfare at ninety.

It would still take nearly five minutes, surface time, to reach Caroline's address.

Two patrol cars screamed through the intersection in their wake, sirens bellowing, lights flashing. Switek reached behind the seat, pulled up a riot shotgun, and pumped a shell into the chamber. Tubbs checked his own loads.

A raggedy dog nearly had a coronary when the line of speeding automobiles screeched and slid around the corner feeding onto the residential street. He scrambled out of the garbage can he had been savaging and hightailed it under the nearest porch.

"I see their car," said Switek, craning over the Corvette's windshield, "but no lights in the house."

Tubbs stomped on the brakes and glided in just as the first bursts of gunfire lit up the windows from inside.

Crockett dropped the telephone and hit the deck just as the assassin stepped from the darkness near the kitchen and cut loose a long burst of automatic fire that raked across the living room, destroying everything at chest level, then returned two feet lower. Gouts of stuffing jumped from holes blown in the sofa. The picture tube of the color TV imploded with a glassine pop and sprayed silver splinters. The stereo turntable danced and jigged as the heavy-caliber slugs ripped it apart; the disc on the platter disintegrated. Caroline's heirloom Chinese vases flew apart into porcelain dust. Large holes tracked across the walls, appearing in magical spurts of lathe and powdered plaster.

Crockett clawed out his .45 and fired several

rounds toward the muzzle flashes of the bigger weapon. But the killer had the advantage, forcing Crockett to scuttle backward while he chopped the living room apart to corner him.

The salvo stopped for a second. Crockett heard the assassin knock out one of his thirty-shot clips and replace it. "Caroline!" he screamed. "Get to the back of the house!" Then he rolled, and placed two bullets into the vestibule light so he was not silhouetted so well. Then he jumped for the hallway. Slugs jump-stitched across the carpeting where he had fallen.

Crockett crashed against the far end of the hallway, knocking apart the antique end table he and Caroline had bought two months after their honeymoon. He saw a dark shape flit past the living-room curtains, briefly shadowed by the outside street lamp. He fired at it, making the drapes dance and the picture window explode into the front lawn. Then, return fire drove him back. He caught a brief glimpse of the killer's face—teeth grit, eyes small and focused behind rectangular glasses—as the brilliant key-light flashes of gunfire lit up the living room.

Crockett was squashed into a ball near the juncture of hallway and kitchen. He smeared the sweat out of his eyes and slammed a new clip into his pistol.

The assassin fired, and the wall came apart three inches above the part in Sonny's hair. He dived into the dining room—to which there was access from both his side and the hitter's side.

This guy is an expert, Sonny thought, panic gripping his guts. *This might be the end.*

"Crockett!" It was Tubbs, outside the house.

"I'm here!" shouted Sonny. "He's inside, near the dining room!"

The front door crashed open, the broken bolt skidding across the floor. Two figures—Tubbs and Switek—ducked back as machine-gun fire tore the threshold molding to shards. Then Tubbs ran in, low, gun-first. The vestibule wall opened up all around him. A large, framed 8 × 10 of the Crocketts' wedding jumped off the wall and smashed on the floor. Other pictures, drilled and perforated, hung, fell, or scraped against the wall like a row of broken teeth.

Crockett saw Caroline and Billy huddled on the floor in the hallway near the bedrooms—just as he saw the killer run for their position. He was stunned that the assassin seemed to know the layout of the house better than he did. Caroline saw him coming and screamed. Crockett tried to track along and pick him off; but he could barely see, and did not wish to plug Caroline by accident.

As Caroline screamed, the killer jumped over her and Billy and piled into the bedroom.

"Sonny . . . ?"

"Come on!" he shouted at Tubbs, and they maneuvered together toward the master bedroom.

Switek, braced against the front door, almost lost his dinner in surprise when the bedroom window flew apart right behind his head.

The killer came somersaulting through, gun-first, and hit the turf, rolling expertly, in a downpour of broken glass and shredded curtains and snapped blinds. He stopped on his feet, his weapon ready—and looked up to see Gina, Trudy, Zito, and four other uniformed officers pointing weapons in his direction.

Switek spun around, hauling his piece up into the firing line.

Crockett and Tubbs appeared in the bedroom window.

The Argentine assassin hesitated for an instant, a look of almost humorous surprise on his face. Then, with something like a rueful sigh and nowhere to run, he fired.

One of the cruiser flashbars exploded. Holes punched across the flanks of the cars. Glass was blown into glittering snow, fiberglass into shredded wheat.

He had surprised everyone by opening fire, and now he continued his efficient destruction by completing his one-eighty turn and leveling his weapon at Crockett.

Crockett's lips whitened and he squeezed off. The hammer of the .45 snapped hollowly on nothing.

The Argentinian fired just as he took four big hits in the back. He folded up, his aim went wild, and the slugs ripped open the ceiling above Crockett's head. Then he spun, jerking, as gunfire tore him completely apart. His steel-rimmed glasses flew away and landed unbroken on the damp grass. The impact of the slugs burrowing into him blew him against the bedroom wall, and he hung onto the windowsill as Crockett and Tubbs dodged out of the path of the incoming gunfire.

When the shooting stopped, the assassin still hung on.

As the cops ran pell-mell across the lawn, Crockett looked down into the face of the killer. His eyes were still open. Feebly, he grabbed Sonny's shirt, leaving an enormous bloodstain. Almost immediately the grip slackened. Pastel-colored blood boiled out of his mouth, his eyes rolled to white, and he died.

And still he hung onto Sonny's shirt.

Crockett backed away. The limp hand disengaged and hung there, the tendons reflexively closing the dead fingers. It was a gruesome sight he would never be able to push out of his mind.

"Caroline . . . ? *Caroline! Billy!*" The spell broke and he dashed back toward the hallway.

Caroline was in shock, still huddled on the floor atop her son, quaking in terror. Billy was whimpering. Crockett felt like whimpering a little himself.

"Shh . . ." he said, holding them. "It's over." But he had told them that before, and it had turned out not to be true. In a very real way, he had betrayed his family; and something more than property had been lost in the last ten minutes.

Then more units screeched to a halt outside, and the ruckus began.

—9—

BULLDOG Bailey Swanson stood a barrel-like five-seven, and was a puffy-cheeked dead ringer for football coach John Madden. Or maybe comedian John Candy. But he did not look too sporting or too amused as he stood in the demolished foyer of Sonny Crockett's house and took in the tableau of destruction.

Absolutely deadpan, he turned to Crockett and said, "It looks like some street gang took a serious dislike to your interior decoration." As he turned, his double-D-size track shoes crunched up pieces of the shattered vestibule mirror. Near his elbow was a staggered line of holes in the wall, each one as big around as a dessert plate. "Anything intact?"

"The bedrooms and bathroom," said Crockett in a monotone. There was little else left. Most of the furniture in the living and dining rooms had been wiped out. Even the silver service inside the buffet cabinet was shot up. One of Billy's stuffed bears had taken a direct hit in the chest; stuffing littered the carpet in a V-shape.

A gory, dried smear of blood marked the bedroom window, along with the bullet holes peppered in all around it. A taped outline on the grass earmarked where the Argentinian hit man had finally collapsed.

It crushed Crockett's heart to see the dull, stunned way Caroline looked around at the ravaged remains of their home. Uniformed officers sifted through the mess. Some photographs were being taken. Newspaper people clustered on the far side of the police barricades. Billy, mercifully, had hustled off to school showing little concern. Children were resilient; it was often the adults who did not bend but snapped. While performing her motherly duties, Caroline had seemed normal, but now her eyes held that terrible lost look.

"Rodriguez is still in intensive care," said Swanson. "The second operation didn't go much better than the first. He's alive, but now they're saying he might have to be hooked up to a machine."

Crockett had moved off, toward Caroline. He took her into Billy's bedroom, one of the few places untouched by the shoot-out. They sat down on his comparatively tiny bed and tried to find truths in each other's eyes.

There was little to see.

He started to speak, but she beat him to it. Curiously, she said, "It's wonderful."

That rocked him. He returned a curious expression.

"It's wonderful to think that you and I could get back together, that we could make it work," she went on. But her eyes were downcast, and she made a point of not touching him. To grasp his hand for reassurance would be to lose control; and for her, right now, that would yield disaster. "But it's wrong for us to keep drifting in and out of each other's lives, Sonny. One of us has got to lock down—and it isn't going to be you. I can tell by the way you go haring off on each assignment. And each time, you court something that could result in what happened here last night. Think of last night multiplied a hundred times."

"But it won't be like that..." he began, then stopped, because he knew he was wrong.

"So it's really the same issue that's always been between us," she said. "The old issues never really die." With a bitter laugh she added, "They don't even fade away much."

"Caroline, this last night, I..."

"It's not last night. Last night was *every* night. It was everything. Don't you see it?"

He drew a long breath and nodded. "I'll give Janet Buckley another call. I'm sure she can reschedule the divorce hearing."

"Lawyers can do anything." She shoved it from her mind, looking around as though seeing the room for the first time. "I've got to get my things together. When Billy gets out of school, we're taking a little trip."

Crockett was about to ask where, then shut his trap. It didn't matter. "Okay." He got up and walked out.

"Tubbs is trying to get you," said Swanson. "On your mobile phone."

Crockett double-timed out to the Corvette. The right side was raked with bullet holes. They had little coronas where the paint had been knocked off around the entry holes. Otherwise, the car was intact: no flats and no engine damage. "Tubbs?"

"Sonny, I need your help to crack Mendez. I scared him when I nearly killed him, and I think he's softening. I want to try to get a fix on Calderone out of him. You game?"

Calderone. The man who had killed Tubbs' brother. The man who'd shot Sonny's marriage all to hell. The man who'd hospitalized Lou Rodriguez and nearly gotten them all murdered. The man who had, by long-distance, shot one of the brass lamps off the *St. Vitus Dance* and scared poor Elvis. Those damned lamps cost money. "What do *you* think, New York?"

Tubbs' strained voice regained some of its wryness. "I think you'll be down here in ten flat."

"Make it eight."

Rudolpho Mendez kept his eyes on the glass as it filled slowly with distilled water so cool it immediately formed beads of condensation on the sides. Against his will, he began to salivate. He'd been bottled up in the interrogation room all night, and it was like the inside of an oven set on "bake." And then, there was this lunatic black cop who seemed ready to come apart at the seams any second. Damned cops were crazier than most of the dopeheads Mendez knew. He hadn't had a drink in six hours, and he was parched. But he couldn't let them see weakness. He hadn't killed anybody. He was convinced that if he could just maintain, he'd do okay. But his composure was fraying. He watched the glass, and *imagined* drinking the water.

Crockett poured. When he finished, Tubbs said, quite civilly, "Where is Calderone?"

Mendez looked doubtfully at Tubbs. When the words *Calderone who?* formed on his lips, Tubbs savagely smashed away the glass when it was an inch in front of Mendez' nose. Mendez flinched. The glass tumbled across the room and shattered on the floor. Cold water soaked into Mendez' pants.

"I have trouble controlling him," said Crockett airily.

Mendez swallowed hard. "He'll kill me if I tell you."

"But my partner here will kill you if you don't," said Crockett. "Seems he's got a score to settle with Calderone that falls outside of what you'd call police jurisdiction. Just keep in mind that we haven't decided whether you died in the shoot-out that killed the hitter."

"Calderone . . ." Mendez shifted nervously. "You've seen how far he can reach."

"Yeah, but he ain't in the room with you right now."

"Did Calderone hire the shooter?" said Tubbs.

Mendez jumped at the sound of Tubbs' voice. "Yeah. Ludovico Paz."

"The Argentinian?" Mendez nodded. "And you were the middleman. You paid Ludovico Paz?"

Mendez nodded again. Now they were getting somewhere. "Why you and not Calderone?"

"Calderone needed someone in the States to monitor Paz. Make sure he did the job and pay him his advance, you know. Help him with whatever he needed. Get him whatever he wanted."

"Like the machine guns? All the hardware he just left behind?"

"Paz smuggled that stuff in himself. Doesn't trust anybody's equipment but his own. Calderone wanted a guy like that."

"You recruited Paz?"

"Calderone would never do a negotiation like that directly. He's never even seen Ludovico Paz."

Tubbs and Crockett exchanged a private look of hope. This could evolve into a real foreign-court advantage. Mendez looked up with a hunted expression. "I want some water now. Please."

"You haven't mentioned where Calderone is," said Tubbs, pouring some for himself and bolting it down.

"You said an advance was paid," said Sonny. "By you to Paz. Tell me about it."

"A cash advance of one hundred thousand in laundered low-denomination currency. U.S. money. Balance due on receipt of the obituaries for the eight names on the hit list. No bodies in basins; Calderone wanted the hits noisy and public, to set an example and bring the other dealers into line."

Crockett did not have to ask if Calderone was planning a comeback.

"Where?" said Tubbs. "Enough screwing around."

While he had been more than talkative about

Ludovico Paz, Mendez' fear cautioned him on the subject of Calderone. Fed up, Tubbs picked up the broken base of the water glass; and as Mendez' eyes widened, stuck it against his throat. Two sharp points of glass caressed his Adam's apple.

"On the other hand," Tubbs said in a threatening rasp barely above a whisper, "I don't have to just kill you. I'll cripple you first. Next I'll march you into a preliminary hearing as an accessory to seven homicides. Then I'll do my damnedest to get you a life sentence, which won't be too hard. And then I'll turn you loose in a federal prison yard with a snitch jacket around your head—and I'll make sure everybody knows where you are."

"I bet he wouldn't make it past his first group-therapy session," said Crockett.

The prospect of getting done over by Tubbs, then killed by Calderone's operatives, was just too much. There was a chance, if these two lunatic cops went after Calderone, that Mendez might somehow be able to crawl away into the woodwork. He grabbed at it. "He's in the Bahamas."

"Over seven hundred islands in that chain, Mendez," Crockett said with a hiss of disappointment. "Guess I'll just have to step out for some air and leave you with Tubbs here."

Trying to regain lost ground, Mendez said, "I'm not his friggin' travel agent, man! That's all he told me!" Off their murderous looks, he tried to use what he knew: "He's opening new supply routes. Shrimpers haul the coke to the islands. From there, cigarette boats bring it here to the mainland. The dealers he had bumped off were taking over his transport routes in the States, and the wholesalers he uses in . . . uh, Cleveland, New York, Detroit, and Chicago. The whole central-northeastern part of his web."

Crockett picked up a manila envelope and spilled a stack of 8 × 10 glossies across the worn and butt-burned table. "Surveillance photos of Calderone," he explained. "Look at them."

Mendez leaned forward and riffled through the pile. Most were grainy telephoto shots of Calderone laughing or eating in backgrounds they all recognized: Colombia, Bogotá, Rio de Janeiro, even Harlequin's in New York. In each of the photos, he was with the same woman—a young, ebony-haired, mocha-skinned lovely.

"All we've got on the woman is that her name is Angelina Medera, age twenty-five, born in Medellin, Colombia. University of São Paolo, then Georgetown. Most recent address, St. Andrews Island . . . in the Bahamas."

"Is this Calderone's woman?" Crockett said.

Indifferently, Mendez shrugged. "Calderone's got women all over the joint; how the hell should I know?"

"We need to know what she is to Calderone. Not a plain hooker, certainly. Mistress? Wife?"

"What are you asking me for? You guys have all the answers—"

Tubbs shoved Crockett out of the way. Even Crockett seemed surprised. "Last chance, middleman!" he snarled. "You don't give me a hook, I start surgery right now."

"Tubbs . . ." Crockett held out a cautioning hand.

"Shut up!" yelled Tubbs. "I'm sick of this bug-eyed scumbone, and I'm gonna carve a Harlem sunset on his face!"

Mendez snapped. "Paz! Paz!" he gibbered. "Paz had the second half of his money coming! He had orders to check in at a hotel under the name of Miller and wait to be contacted once the hit list was finished!"

"What hotel, where?" said Crockett.

"Conch Bay Lodge on St. Andrews Island. That's all I know, I swear to God."

It was all they needed. Tubbs said, "Give the man a sip of *agua*."

"How's your Spanish?" asked Swanson, who watched Mendez gulping water through the one-way glass.

"Está bueno," said Crockett, reholstering his automatic and stowing extra clips in the shoulder pockets.

"Listen, guys, I've got a lot of doubts about this," said the captain. "It isn't exactly on the up-and-up, any more than your little interrogation was."

"Phew," said Crockett. "Mad Dog Tubbs. You even had me worried with that little scenario in there, pal."

Tubbs' gaze was flat and hard. "Maybe it wasn't an act." That deflated some of the mirth in the room.

"Save it," said Swanson. "The long and the short is this: you guys volunteer to go bashing off to the Bahamas, we're not responsible if you get your butts shot off."

"Understood," said Crockett.

"All we can do is notify the local authorities and

ask for assistance in extraditing Calderone—*if* he's down there."

"He's there," said Tubbs. "I know it. I can feel it inside me."

"We have absolutely no jurisdiction down there. And you two aren't the most objective choices for this little mission, now, are you?" The lack of response was all the answer Swanson needed. "But Lou Rodriguez is a friend of mine. Damned good poker player. And he highly recommends you—that much I know from your files. But while you're out on this limb, I'm responsible for everything you do. And there's one news item I want to make nice and sparkling clear: I saw Sonny's house. And I heard from Milch, over at Division, that Calderone was responsible for killing your brother, Tubbs."

"You heard right."

"All right. So here's the scoop: I do not, repeat, do *not* want to see or hear anything that is not textbook police procedure. You guys are there for surveillance only—no vigilante crap. The only place Calderone gets the seat of his pants nailed to a wall is in a Miami courtroom. You dig?"

They both nodded and grabbed their coats to leave.

"I can't hear you," Swanson said with a cobra smile.

"Yes, sir," said Crockett stiffly. Tubbs did likewise.

"And Crockett? I want a full report on Mendez typed and on my desk before you go anyplace, don't I?"

Crockett was caught short. "Uh . . . yes, you do. Sir."

Swanson smiled. "Go now." He waved them out.

They walked a few paces down the corridor in silence; then Tubbs said, "Guy's a real hump-buster, huh?"

"He is, at that," said Crockett. "The iron fist in the velvet glove. I like it."

Before Crockett began typing his narrative on Mendez, he made a phone call to someone named Sammy Rheingold.

"Sammy who?"

"A little surprise," said Crockett, a smoke dangling from one corner of his mouth as he typed. "How long will it take you to get ready for a trip to the Bahamas, Tubbs?"

He held out his hands. "I've been ready ever since I came to Miami."

—10—

SAMMY Rheingold had blue and red biker's tattoos running up one arm and down the other. He chain-smoked Camels and often balanced them off with a toothpick. He wore chinos, motorcycle boots, and a torn, faded Mötley Crüe T-shirt ripped in at least a dozen places. His arms were black to the elbows with grease and oil, and his blond hair seemed to be slicked back with a fifty-fifty cut of Brylcream and car lube. His claim to fame was a distant relation to the man responsible for Rheingold—the beer—which was sometimes hard to come by in Miami.

"Gotta practically friggin' import it," he said around his cigarette, arms sunk into the engine well of Crockett's speedboat. From the deck of the *St. Vitus Dance*, Elvis watched the goings-on with reptilian uninterest.

Crockett hurled a chocolate-sprinkle doughnut

deck-to-deck, and the alligator caught it in his toothy doorway of a mouth. "Tell me about fast, oh wizard," he said.

Sammy slugged from his can of lukewarm brew. "With the new carbs and lifters . . . hell, you'll be able to outrun anything short of a Bell chopper, and I don't mean a sickle."

"Sickle?" said Tubbs, stepping gingerly around Elvis on the opposite boat.

"Motorcycle, to you black New York folk," Crockett specified. "As in *moto-sickle.*"

Sammy scraped curls of clotted grease from his arms, searching for his wristwatch. "To hell with it; it don't matter what time it is." With a perverse grin, he added, "I ain't even gonna ask what you dudes are up to." He slammed and dogged down the engine cover and began to stow his tools.

"Thanks for the house call, Sammy."

"S'nothing. You owe me one, right? The great thing about you, Sonny, is you always make good. This baby gives you any grief, phone me day or night—but you won't have to, I know, because you're messin' with the best!"

"Hallelujah," intoned Crockett. They laughed and shook hands, Crockett getting his thoroughly blackened.

"See what I mean?" Sammy said to Tubbs. "Dude don't mind gettin' his hands dirty! Dude's *righteous!*"

Tubbs hefted an enormous seabag across the water to Crockett. "Yeah. Dude's bad, too, and raw, and buffed."

"Exactly!" cried Sammy as he headed off down the dock.

To Crockett, Tubbs added, "Sammy is in orbit somewhere around Neptune."

Crockett lifted the seabag; it took both hands. "Pretty weighty for a carry-on."

Tubbs feigned indifference. "Just some flares and binoculars and . . . stuff."

Crockett dumped it out on the deck of the cigarette boat, nodding in agreement. "Kevlar vests and body armor, M-845 Nitefinder scopes, a couple of Heckler-Koch machine pistols, tear gas . . . what looks like about two thousand rounds of ammo. Yeah, I'd say it was your basic surveillance gear, Tubbs."

"A good boy scout is always prepared."

"In addition to my gun, your gun, the sniper rifles in the hold, the M16 mounted behind the door, and your little family-heirloom shotgun, am I right?"

He shrugged theatrically. "Life insurance."

Crockett jumped across to squat before Elvis for a heart-to-heart, one knee on either side of the beast's knobby, olive-drab prow. "Okay, pal," he said, "no goin' berserk while I'm gone now, y'hear? No dropping in on the Panamanian vice consul's receptions, no scaring the snowbirds, no scarfing up the fishermen's catch of the day. No eating the clock. Sonny *needs* his clock."

The alligator listened with what looked like rapt, stoned fascination. Then he yawned open his hinged face and belched. Fearing the worst, Crockett muttered, "Oh no," and rechecked the cabin on the *St. Vitus Dance*.

Twenty dollars' worth of digital Nichimita alarm clock—with snooze button and AM-FM—had been consumed.

"You worthless monster," Crockett said half-heartedly. "See?" he said to Tubbs. "I'm outta his sight two days, I leave him a baby-sitter and plenty of DogNips—and this is how he thanks me."

"Elvis doesn't kill time. He eats it, right?"

"Yeah." He gave the gator what he hoped was a dour glare. "Behave. That's an order. Uncle Ernie will be by with your breakie around eight—okay?"

Elvis affirmed that this was acceptable.

Crockett jumped across to the cigarette boat and keyed the ignition. "We're not back in a week or so," he called to Elvis, "the boat's all yours!"

Tubbs tossed off the mooring lines, and Crockett puttered out toward the open sea, building speed. Moping, Elvis watched them go. He hated long good-byes.

"So why the mechanic?" Tubbs said over the growl of the engines. "This thing need a tune-up?"

"Nope," said Crockett as the boat booked along steadily. "I'll show you why the mechanic." He rammed the throttle forward, and the prow of the boat lifted out of the water as the engines went instantaneously from a purr to a roar. Tubbs was mashed into his seat by the acceleration. The boat skimmed along like a rocket.

"How fast does this thing go, anyway?" Tubbs asked, hanging onto his armrests.

"A lot faster than it did when you first stole it from me," Crockett said loftily. He was getting high on the sheer forward motion. "About a million knots."

St. Andrews Island was an hour away.

The sea was wide-open all around them; Crockett felt an almost disorienting sense of freedom and lateral mobility. When he looked again at the passenger seat, he realized that Tubbs did not share this romantic viewpoint.

"You look a little green around the intake valves, my man," he shouted across the salt spray.

Tubbs had tried to navigate back to the beer cooler. He hoped a brew would settle his panic and take his mind away from the lurching motion of the boat. He felt fragile out here in the middle of this choppy-watered nowhere. "I feel like I'm about to ralph into your nice ocean," he said. "This boating garbage is for the birds."

"Aha! A city boy at heart."

Tubbs managed a grin. "Gotta have that pulsating New York asphalt under my Guccis, ace. Closest I ever got to open water before was the fountain at Lincoln Center."

Crockett reached under the seat and tossed a towel at his partner, who had slotted his beer into a cup-holder and was now fumbling with a map. "Relax! We'll be there in twenty minutes."

"Yeah, right. All I see is blue. I look up—blue. Down—blue again. And this map—more blue." As he tried to show the map to Crockett, it was ripped from his hands and blown overboard. Lost at sea forever. "See what I mean?" he said helplessly. Pointing over his shoulder, he continued,

"Only thing on that map was little *blue* dots. How can you be so sure we'll hit one? They're microscopic! What if we pass right on by and wind up in Portugal or someplace?"

Crockett grinned wickedly. "No chance. We'll run out of gas long before we hit Portuguese waters."

"Thanks." Tubbs rolled his eyes. "I'll just call you Ishmael. I'll bet there's sharks out here, too. Sharks . . . and them weird-looking flat things, with spines and luminous eyeballs, that only come up at night after people run out of petrol . . . octopuses and things with *suckers* . . . euuggh."

"Maybe worse," said Crockett, enjoying himself immensely.

"What are you talking about?"

"Well . . . we're right smack in the middle of the Bermuda Triangle. Did you know that?"

Tubbs made a hissing noise of despair. "Sharks and weirdness," he said with his hand on his head.

Crockett pointed ahead. "See that white dot?"

"Where?"

"About two o'clock starboard."

"Gimme that in English."

"Over there. That's Bimini. And St. Andrews."

"Terrific. Out of the pan and into the flame broiler. All we have is no backup, a long-shot cover story, and a snapshot of Calderone's main squeeze." Then he settled. "Come to think of it, what are we waiting for?"

"That's the seafaring spirit," said Crockett.

"Ain't got nothin' to do with the sea," Tubbs returned as the dot grew to a speck, to a lump, to a mountained castaway island interrupting the smooth blue curve of the horizon. He was thinking about his brother, Rafael.

The Conch Bay Lodge was a typically well-to-do Bahamian retreat, its private dock filled up with an eclectic array of boats. There was an outdoor registration desk. And a bar overhung with dry palm fronds and duded up with shells, fishnetting, petrified starfish, glass globes, and other seafaring rickrack.

Crockett slotted the boat smoothly into place—he *was* a good helmsman, Tubbs reflected—and together they hauled their sling bags and canvas duffels up a salt-rotted, timbered stairway toward the bar.

The barman patiently observed their ascent. His eyes were blazingly blue, with that slightly burned-out shine seen in surfers and lovers of hashish. Jimbo Spitz—formerly Jimmy Schwarzenspitznikopf—was both. His hair was fine brown, eternally uncombed and windblown. It looked natural on him. His mug was tanned, with flaking skin on the bridge of his red nose. Jimbo enjoyed the hell out of getting high on life—but was not adverse to frequent artificial enhancers to his natural high.

"You checking in?"

Crockett nodded, and a beaming Jimbo produced a couple of already prepared drinks in hollowed-out coconuts, with long red straws extending from them.

"Compliments of the *casa,*" he said with a friendly, silly-stupid tilt of the head. He was like a big, affectionate, slobbery cocker spaniel. "This here is a Jimbo Special. The rum in it kills the lousy taste. So . . . you guys here for the diving, or the windsurfing regatta?"

"Strictly rest and recreation," said Tubbs, uncomfortable with the surroundings.

"Yeah, recreation you'll get plenty of." Jimbo grinned. "But rest? Not when we're kicking off the Junkaroo."

"What the hell is . . . ?"

"Junkaroo Festival, man! Like Mardi Gras. Masks, costumes, drinkin' and dancin' in the streets—four days of nonstop weirdness. Didn't you ever see *Thunderball?*" He jittered off to deal with a customer at the far end of the bar.

"Nonstop weirdness," muttered Tubbs. "Just what I need."

Leaning in close, Crockett said, "You'd better drop it a notch, buddy. You're strung way too tight."

Sipping his Jimbo Special, Tubbs returned, "Why don't we just take care of business fast-like, so we don't have to worry about anything—like whether anybody at the Robinson Crusoe Inn here has ever seen Ludovico Paz before. If Calderone isn't on the island, I don't care to stick around for the Junkyard Festival, you dig?"

Crockett shook his head. "You gotta develop a positive attitude, son. Want some food?"

Tubbs lightened up. "Yeah, I am a bit hungry, now that we're off the boat."

"Just remember the old saying, Tubbs—'When in St. Andrews . . .'"

"Yeah. Right."

Jimbo rock-and-rolled back to them. "Any-who, like I was sayin', you guys are gonna love this place.

Beautiful women, water sports, nightclubs, unlimited beach frontage." Conspiratorially, he added, "You need anything, you see the kid. I can snare you some Jamaican ganja that'll tie-dye your frontal lobes in Technicolor, man."

Crockett sighed. "Maybe later."

Shrugging, he said, "Smart. I got into some Caribbean weed when I came down here for my spring break—and missed my plane back to the mainland."

"How long ago was spring break?" said Tubbs.

Jimbo had to think about it. "Uh . . . seven years, last April. Lemme get your bags checked in. Hey, Luis!"

A nut-brown islander started over, but Crockett headed him off. "It's okay. We'll handle 'em." It wouldn't do to have their arsenal spill out all over the patio. "Reservations are under the name of Miller, Luis. Find out if there've been any messages for me yet."

Luis *yessir*ed and ran off.

"Let's polish these off," said Crockett. "I'll check in with the chief of police; you see what you can get on the woman."

"Why not try Jimbo, who can do anything?"

"Yeah, why not?" Luis reappeared and informed Crockett that there had been no messages for Miller. Presumably—now that someone had checked into the room—Calderone would be notified that it was time to make the final payment to Ludovico Paz—aka Miller.

Tubbs pulled out one of the snaps of Angelina Medera with Calderone.

When Jimbo saw the photo, his face increased its normal wattage by half. "I knew you dudes were up to something." He grinned. "What can I help ya with?"

"Friend of a friend in New York," said Tubbs.

With confident understanding, Jimbo nodded. "Whatever you say, man. It's cool. Every third person through here has got something cooking. It's the way of the islands—mystery, foreign intrigue."

Tubbs tucked a Jackson note behind the photo and slid it across the bar. "Ever see her?"

"Angelina? That's an easy one. Teaches school up at the north end of the island. Stone fox. Talented, too. She painted that." He hooked his thumb toward the back of the bar. Hanging there was a painting of a solitary woman in white, standing alone on a beach, gazing out at the sea. The composition, with its blocky anatomy and bright tropical tones, brought to mind Gauguin; but there was something inherently lonely in the picture as well—a depiction of isolation in the midst of gaiety. Tubbs' eyes lingered on the canvas.

"Know where I can find her?" he said.

Jimbo smiled. "Like I say, it's a small island."

Sidney Albury was a capable, easygoing sort of man, the kind that wields as much control as he can, calmly and without drawing attention to his skill. His curly black hair was cropped into a sort of flattop and looked almost military; his broad West Afrikaans face was brooding and Buddha-like. He did not perspire in the afternoon heat. His close-fitting police khakis seemed starched and unsullied by human sweat.

He placed two cups of strong Colombian coffee down on his desk, one for himself and one for Crockett. There was an air conditioner in the office, but it wasn't running.

"We have had no reports on Francisco Calderone in quite some time," Albury said slowly, as if making his word choices from a catalogue. His voice had the musical island lilt that Crockett associated with homegrown reggae music. "We try to keep an eye on the major traffickers, of course—but with over seven hundred islands, uncountable inlets, private coves, and landing strips, it is an almost impossible task."

"I appreciate your problem," Sonny said, tasting the coffee. It was very strong, and very good.

"I assure you that if a criminal of Calderone's stature came to my island, I would be the first to know. It is a small world here. If there is any change of status, I will of course notify you straight away at your hotel. In the meantime, rest assured that I and my department are at your disposal during your stay here. I am most anxious to cooperate with the mainland law-enforcement officials in bringing criminals to justice." He drank his entire cupful of coffee in one long swallow.

"Thank you." Crockett was disappointed. Albury was open, patient, and helpful—and of less real value than Jimbo Spitz. The man talked as if his speech had been prepared, like a walking, talking press release for island law enforcement.

As Crockett rose to leave, Albury said, "By the way, where is your partner?"

Crockett had not mentioned the small detail that he was posing as Calderone's hit man to receive a payoff—merely that he and Tubbs were searching for Calderone. And now he did not feel like giving away anything on Tubbs, either, so he told a lie that was the truth, in its elegant simplicity. "My partner's gone fishing," he said.

He wondered if Tubbs had caught anything.

—11—

TUBBS hung back in the foliage for a time. He wanted to study the woman first, to try to pick up vibrations about her.

She stood on the expanse of clean white beach midway between where the palms stopped and the sea began. There was an enormous luxury yacht anchored some distance out, past the reefs, and she was looking up periodically in its direction while she painted. Tubbs thought, though, that she did not choose to see the boat. It was the ocean that interested her. The beach was deserted for several New York city blocks to his left and right, and she had her back to him.

Angelina Medera was on the tall side, Tubbs saw, about five-nine. Her facial bone structure had elements of the aristocratic that were revealed when he used the binoculars: almost aggressively high cheekbones, a substantial chin (or rather, Tubbs thought, a chin that did not melt away and make the face look weak), a wide, generous mouth. Her nose was broad, keeping the face from looking too blandly beautiful—the face of a real person, and not a photo-perfect cover girl. Her face held strong character buffered by a degree of childlike naïveté. Tubbs assumed this was a result of two warring bloodlines crashing together to produce this child. He could see a princess there, but also a lovely peasant girl. Her dark, elliptical eyes rejoiced in the things they saw.

She daubed at the rectangular seascape half-finished on the easel before her, unconsciously posing as she leaned back to inspect her work and forward to add to it. When she lifted her foot, Tubbs could see the lighter skin on the soles of her feet; the rest of her was a calm mocha brown. West Indies mix or South American stock, he estimated. She was possessed of a cloud of wavy ink-black hair that fell heavy and full to the waistline of her white sundress and was stirred by the sea breeze.

She matched up with the photograph in Tubbs' pocket, but only in the most elementary sense. She was much more attractive, but even telephoto surveillance photography did not dim her full radiance. Her face seemed to change contexts for Tubbs; he had to remind himself that this was Calderone's whore, one of his kept women, something that could at last be turned against the bastard that killed Tubbs' brother.

He angled out of the bushes and approached, his city heels biting deeply into the sand, which was more like fine white powder. It reminded him of snow. He slung the binocular case over one shoulder, and affixed the lower button on his light summer jacket so it wouldn't hang open and reveal his pistol at the wrong moment. He was wearing one of his open-collared silk shirts. The Kid was a killer this afternoon.

Fine white powder, he thought. The weird irony of it hit him just as she turned around. He was ten feet away, and still she did not notice him, so intent was she on her painting. But in the moment she turned, he could see her face, up close, for real, the first time, and that caused another odd thought:

She's beautiful. What am I doing here . . . ?

There was a smudge of yellow oil paint on her thumb. She smeared it on a riotously colored apron tucked into the belt of her sundress. She squinted at the painting, then dabbed some pigments together.

"It reminds me of a Cuban painter," he said. "Vacherrez."

She did not jump. She turned again, slowly now, to see him, and he got the creepy feeling she had known she was being watched all along. With a modest smile, she said, "I don't know if I'm more surprised by your sudden appearance—or that a *tourista* would be acquainted with Vacherrez."

Tubbs made sure she saw that his gaze was on her work, and not on the body suggested by the gentle curvature and fall of the dress. "He and Colican are two of my favorite Caribbean artists." He counted himself lucky that he remembered to say Ca-*rib*-ean and not Cari-*bee*-an.

She seemed to accept this, saying nothing further.

"Ahh . . . actually, I'm down here on sort of a buying trip," he said. "I own a gallery in SoHo. I'd be very interested in seeing more of your work."

She made him wait a moment for it. "I'm flattered—but I only give them away to friends. I've never sold one."

He caught her gaze and held it; it seemed to be a struggle for him. "In that case, I absolutely hope to have one."

A small motor launch puttered away from the distant yacht and began its slow progress toward the shore. She heard its engine and broke her eye contact with Tubbs to turn and look. "I have to go." She slotted the easel into her art case and began to collect her painting things.

The threat of losing the moment impelled him to step forward and gently grab her arm. She jostled her easel; only Tubbs saw her antique Cartier wristwatch fall into the fine sand. "You can't go," he said.

Her expression told him she was very unused to being handled by insistent men. She gave a slight, noncommittal tug. He held. "And why can't I?" she said, her eyes on the nearing shuttle launch.

Tubbs cranked up the charm to full gain. "Because there's an old Buddhist custom that specifies if karmic fate causes you to cross paths with someone who is a major knockout, they must consent to be your honored guest for dinner and dancing at this terrific café I heard was up at Lyford Cay."

The tension broke when she smiled. "That's a very liberal interpretation of Buddhist philosophy."

"That's the advantage of Buddhism; it's adaptable." He smiled and she returned it. "Tell me your name . . . ?"

"Angelina."

"Mine's Richard."

There was the slightest pressure of her hand against his. "I've really got to go now . . . Richard."

He nodded and stepped to the easel to help her pack up. As he did, he crushed the watch into the sand with his foot, gently. The launch had now coasted up to a short dock some forty yards distant. Using the little time he had left, he decided to test her a little. "That your boyfriend out on that yacht?"

"Should I call you the Man of a Thousand Questions?" she teased.

"Just one more: will I see you again?"

The launch pilot was visibly impatient. But she tarried an extra moment to appraise Tubbs. "It's possible." She punctuated this with a genuine smile.

He carried her easel and art case to the boat. The pilot was a lanky Brazilian who glared at Tubbs. She waved as he slogged back up the beach; and when he turned for a last look, she was seated in the launch, her attention on the yacht.

When the boat had dwindled away to toy size, he stooped to retrieve the watch. Sand sprinkled from it. He dropped it around his fingers, examining it as he plodded back up toward the tree line.

"Why, you silver-tongued New Yorker devil, you." It was Crockett standing in Tubbs' hiding place, another pair of binoculars strapped around his neck. He had observed all or most of what had transpired. "How'd you make out?"

"Like a bandit." He pocketed the watch. "You?"

"Nada. Mis-tuh Chief Albury says he has not seen hide nor hair of Calderone in months. But there's something about the way he says it that sets off alarms in my head."

"Like he might've checked with Calderone on the phone before making his statement?"

"Something like that. Although Albury looks too upstanding to be in Calderone's pocket. That doesn't mean he might not . . . y'know, look the other way if two foreign vice cops had an accident."

"That makes my day," Tubbs said, eyes on the yacht. He scanned it with his own field glasses. "If she has anything to do with him, he'll be back around this way eventually. If not now, tomorrow; if not then, the next day. I can feel it."

Crockett's brow creased in annoyance. "You want to explain these voodoo hunches you keep getting about Calderone? Hell, Tubbs—that guy could be anywhere. He's probably got fifty houses around the globe. South America, South Africa, anywhere in Europe. He hasn't stayed alive this long being predictable."

"Oh yeah?" said Tubbs, handing across his binoculars. "Don't underestimate a man's weak spots. Take a look."

Crockett grabbed the glasses and focused. He saw Angelina being helped out of the launch by the boatman. When she was on deck, she drifted into the embrace of a short man with curly, silver-black hair. Even at this distance, Crockett's memory filled in the pockmarks on the man's face, the ratty little mustache, the teeth with the spaces between them.

He whistled air between his teeth. "Hot *damn* . . . it's him!" The excitement of the chase whooshed up in him. "We'll get the boat's registry, watchdog the harbors to see where he puts in, then give Swanson a call. . . ."

Tubbs' face had gone flat and cold, all the charm gone. His stare toward the yacht—without glasses—was murderous.

Calming, Crockett said, "Hey, buddy, you're not in the process of forgetting you're a cop, are you? You and I are gonna go by the book." There was no immediate response. "Aren't we?"

"You mean the way we did last time? When we wound up standing on a runway in the middle of the night, your car and my arm busted, watching this scuzzwad fly away with a big grin on his face and ten million clear in some Swiss account? The guy who had your house shot to scrap lumber just the other morning?"

Tubbs was edging onto marshy ground by purposefully pushing Sonny's angry buttons. It was true—Calderone had run up an enormous bill with both of them. Crockett's marriage and Tubbs' brother were just two lines on that bill. Lou Rodriguez, hanging by a thread in a hospital back in Miami, was a third.

"Listen to me." Crockett was adamant without getting ticked off. "If you can't keep a lid on that vigilante impulse of yours, then just hand over the badge right now and blow him away on your own, as a citizen. Otherwise, get one thing straight. We're here to catch him and deport him, preferably without any holes in him, pure and simple."

"Simple," said Tubbs. "Maybe not so pure. I'm up to follow the agenda, Crockett. I'll play by the rules one more time where Calderone is concerned. But if this starts to slip into an instant replay of last time . . . then I'm gonna take him down. And nothing is gonna stand in my way—not you, not Albury, not that overeducated hooker, or anyone else."

Then he turned and huffed away.

"Tubbs!" It was useless. Sonny decided to let Tubbs simmer for a while.

By the time the sun had set and risen again, there were still no messages left for Miller at the Conch Bay Lodge. Calderone was not discussed, but Tubbs cooled off after using most of that evening for a long, introspective walk around town, watching preparations for the Junkaroo parade and festivities.

When Crockett awakened, he was alone in the room. Tubbs had left a note saying that breakfast would be brought up at nine. It was a quarter till.

Crockett rolled from his bed and, naked except for a pair of boxer shorts, began groaning and chuffing through a progression of Marine push-ups. He'd hit thirteen when the front door opened, footsteps approached, and a day-old edition of the Miami *Herald* thwacked the floor, raising dust in front of his nose. A droplet of sweat cut loose from the tip of his nose and hit the subheadline in the second column, below the fold.

DETECTIVE KILLED

SUSPECTED DRUG HIT

" 'The latest in an alleged series of drug-related murders in the greater Miami area was a high-ranking Dade County vice officer, shot to death yesterday in his South Beach home by unknown assailants. Details on the identity of the officer have not yet been released . . . blah, blah, blah . . . suspects in custody will be arraigned . . . possible contract killings . . . blah, blah . . .' "

"Suspects?" Tubbs snorted. "What suspects? What if Calderone reads this and thinks Ludovico Paz is dead—which he is?"

"Reverse strategy, my dear Tubbs. Calderone knows how the police operate. The FBI usually gets their man on the TV news; whenever some lunatic starts chopping up waitresses with a meat cleaver, they make sure to specify on the evening news that a suspect has been caught, and they always give him some easily digestible personality quirk so the viewing public will decide there is no killer at large to disturb their sleep. They'll bring in a guy they say is a former chef, for example. Or they'll say the guy was poor and romantically estranged. The usual official b.s.—but it works. And it preserves the illusion that the police are always in control."

"So by suggesting that Ludovico Paz was caught, and not naming names . . ."

"Calderone will be fairly certain that Paz *hasn't* been caught, and that the authorities are just covering it up. Simple and elegant, isn't it? Besides, I can take this in with the other clippings as my last obituary when I pick up the hit fee."

"You're in pretty good shape for a dead man. And you made the front page, to boot."

Crockett grimaced, sitting up. "I don't think my mother would be anxious to read this, though."

"Any word for Miller yet?"

"Lots of nothing. I pounded on the door of your bungalow for a good five minutes last night."

"What was up?" said Tubbs.

"Just me and a couple of cold beers with no place to go."

"I took a walk. A long one. Trying to sort things out, y'know?"

Crockett nodded.

"I'll be fine—as soon as we take care of what we came here for." He was distracted by distant singing, growing closer. "What's . . . ?"

"Sounds like an a cappella rendition of Led Zeppelin," said Crockett. "Off-key. Which could only mean . . ."

Jimbo Spitz poked his head over the porch rail. A huge silver tray of food was perched on one shoulder. *"And sheeeez biii-ying a stairwayyyyy to* . . . Good mornin', gents! Breakfast has arrived!" He set the tray down with a crash on the porch table, vaulted over the rail, and bopped into the room. Jimbo was speeding on more than coffee this fine island morning. "What's on the old aye-genda this *bee-yoo-ti-fool* day? Hey, man—I can lay a couple of doobie-doobs on ya. You can kick back, soak up the rays, do the whole island trip, right? Scuba-fishing, para-sailing . . . Hey! Up and at 'em. No appetites? Mind if I have a piece of toast?"

Crockett rolled his eyes. "Sure."

Jimbo grabbed a slice and piled some of Crockett's scrambled eggs on top of it. Then he made a circuit of the room, waving his free hand, talking with his mouth full. "Say, dudes, I'm taking the day off from writing, you know? An author should never even go in the same time zone as a typewriter when there are southerly trade winds. I can't invest my characters with any humanity when the air gets like this. I sat down to type, and the first *word* had a mistake in it. Typos are always a bad omen. So I gave it up. Tomorrow's another day, right?"

This performance amused both detectives. "What are you writing, Jimbo?" Crockett asked.

Jimbo wolfed down half the toast in one bite. "Mmm . . . novel. It's about half finished. The rest of it is locked away safely up here." He tapped his temple. "But I have got it up to two thousand, one hundred and twenty-seven pages so far."

"How long you been working on it?"

"Mmphh . . . five years. Catch this." He cleared his throat and struck a self-consciously Shakespearean pose. "'The house was built on the highest part of the narrow tongue of land between the harbor and the open sea. It had lasted through three hurricanes and was built solid as a ship . . .'"

"I'm impressed," said Tubbs, who was.

"You oughta be! It's Hemingway." Jimbo was totally zoned out. "Now, I'm working on a sort of contemporary island classic in the *mold* of old Papa. It's kind of a cross between *Mutiny on the Bounty* and *Road Warrior,* with bits from *Beat Street* and *On Golden Pond* thrown in. Very commercial, but artistic at the same time, y'know?"

"Sounds like a surefire best-seller," said Crockett.

"Yeah, and then, after the money starts comin' in

from the book," Jimbo added, "maybe I'll buy this place." He shoved another piece of toast into his mouth and a backup piece into his shirt pocket. "Catch you dudes later. Oh, wow, almost forgot—" He yanked a battered envelope out of his trouser pocket. It looked as though he might have slept on it. "For Miller."

Jimbo and his repertoire of tunes receded into the brush as Crockett slit open the envelope and said, "Bingo." He waved the slip of paper inside. "Got a meet with Calderone's man at the Typhoon House, a café near here. Final payment for the dead hit man. I figured he read the newspapers."

Tubbs spot-checked his shoulder holster. "Need backup?"

"No. This one's better if I go solo. Typhoon House is in the middle of town; I doubt if they'll try anything. They don't have any reason to pull any stunts."

"Good," Tubbs said. "This'll give me an opportunity to cultivate my little romance."

Crockett scoffed. "Ah-huh. Despite your obvious charms and animal sexual magnetism, just how do you know she'll even see you again?"

"I got a feeling," Tubbs said with a secret grin.

–12–

TYPHOON House was less phony than some of the other tourist traps on the island—less bamboo decor, fewer mixed drinks with straws and umbrellas. Here, a quiet clique of serious afternoon drinkers filed in and out, sucking up their shots and beers and maybe catching some sports action on the black-and-white TV above the bar. The barman was a Big Kahuna type in the extra-large range. He methodically polished the mahogany bartop with practiced swipes of the worn cloth in his massive fist, as he had been doing for years. The bar, despite cigarette burns, gouges, and stains, shone like black glass. He said nothing when Crockett rolled in, ordered a stiff shot of Jack Daniel's and a beer chaser, and slapped down his money.

In a booth in the cool dimness beyond the entrance, Crockett blew down the raw whiskey and followed it with a long slug from the brown bottle. Fire and ice. Maybe drinking so early in the day was a bad idea—the act held too many unpleasant memories, some of which Caroline had a supporting role in—but he was slipping on his assassin's mask now, and it made him feel the part, tough and bristly.

And just in time, he saw. A short man had entered Typhoon House—a short man in a pressed white linen suit. He moved with a dancer's grace through the door and scanned the interior of the bar. He was holding a largish leather briefcase bound in stainless steel. He whipped off his wraparound sunglasses, then headed over to Crockett's booth. Crockett was strategically placed with his back to the rear wall.

The stranger approached Crockett directly. "Are you an American?" Up close Crockett could see the man's left eye was milky and dead. Must've caught a shiv or an ice pick.

"Name's Miller." Sonny did not extend his hand.

"Guillermo Pino." The Colombian killer slid into the booth opposite him. "Are you enjoying your stay on the island, Mr. . . . Miller?"

"What, are you from the board of tourism?" Crockett responded coldly. "Cut the questionnaire and let's get down to business."

Pino nodded. "Business. At least you act like an American." A snakelike half-smile wriggled across his unpleasant face.

Crockett pulled a manila envelope from beneath his new, broad-brimmed Panama hat. He slid it across the polished wood. "Press clippings, Miami *Herald*. Seven obituaries." He threw in the paper Tubbs had shown him earlier. "Number eight's on page one."

Pino spared the envelope and paper the briefest glance. He slid the briefcase across. "One hundred thousand American. Nice doing business with you."

Crockett pushed the briefcase back across. This brought a look of mild surprise to Pino's scarred and ugly face. "We're not done doing business yet," he said, low and deadly. He tapped the clippings with a finger. "My prices are based on standards. Rudolpho Mendez omitted telling me that James Crockett was a vice cop. My price for that kind of job is the same as for military attachés and politicos, because the heat is more intense. Is Calderone trying to play some kind of stupid bargain-basement game with me?"

Pino stiffened, but held firm.

"You still owe me an extra thirty thousand for that last job," Crockett said.

Pino's expression changed little. "Señor Calderone never renegotiates."

Crockett smiled and fired up a cigarette with his Zippo paratrooper's lighter, flicking the shell back and thumbing the wheel in a one-handed motion. "This is not a renegotiation," he said calmly through a cloud of gray tobacco smoke. "This is not even a *ne*-gotiation. Señor Calderone either pays the proper fee for the job he ordered . . . or I take up the slack for him."

"Meaning?" Pino's mien was that of a market haggler who preferred more gullible customers.

"Meaning that the hit list doesn't have to stop at eight. Señor Calderone could easily become number nine. Tell him—politely—that he should pay his bills."

Pino digested this new input and regained his composure. His stony killer's face slid back into position. "Possibly some new arrangement can be made."

"The only thing you have to arrange is delivery by sundown. No more Mickey Mouse."

Pino rose stiffly. "I will convey your message to him."

Crockett butted his smoke in the shot glass. "And tell Calderone I'm through dealing with errand boys. Mendez got himself busted and nearly blew my cover; you don't look too much smarter. In Argentina, money that gets paid for blood gets paid personally. By him. Tonight."

"I understand completely," said Pino, picking up the briefcase. He glided out of Typhoon House without a farewell or a sound.

Crockett left two minutes afterward. He needed an espresso to settle his churning stomach.

The tiny island schoolhouse was a quaint, romantic one-room affair, well maintained and well away from the tourist paths. It was brightly painted and looked like a set from a movie.

As Tubbs walked carefully up the inclined pathway to the structure's front stoop, he began to hear Angelina's musical, lightly accented voice drifting down from an open window. She was reciting "Madeline."

"In an old house in Paris
That was covered in vines,
Lived twelve little girls in two straight lines . . ."

Tubbs moved to a window and saw that Angelina's charges were an even dozen youngsters, not too well dressed, but dark, healthy, totally adorable, with black button eyes fixed in fascinated attention as they listened to her read.

"In two straight lines
They broke their bread,
And brushed their teeth
And went to bed..."

She spotted him standing outside, at which point he produced her watch from his pocket and held it up. The children could not see Tubbs from her angle. She pondered for a moment, still reading, and then nodded in the direction of the classroom door. Her voice faded as Tubbs moved around the building.

"'They smiled at the good, and...' Theresa, would you please continue reading to the class?"

Theresa rose shyly and accepted the book at the place Angelina indicated. Then, as if the greatest honor had been bestowed upon her, Theresa began to read—haltingly at first, but with swiftly accumulating verve. Angelina watched tolerantly until the little girl hit her stride, then smiled and ducked quickly outside.

"I'm surprised to see you," she said, her face open and bright.

"I'm pleased to see you again so soon," said Tubbs. "I asked at the hotel where I might return this, and they sent me up here. This is quite charming."

She accepted the watch with undisguised happiness. "I was afraid I'd never see it again. I don't usually take it off. Was it at the beach?" She closed it up in her hand; her genuine joy knocked Tubbs off balance. How could this warmly pretty schoolmarm be the main squeeze for somebody like Calderone? Yet, he'd seen them on the boat yesterday. "This is a family heirloom," she said, bringing him back to the here and now.

Silence fell between them—a second that Tubbs had to fill: "And since we missed dinner yesterday, I thought I'd try you for lunch today . . . ?"

She seemed to have an instant problem with that, as though she'd known he was going to ask. Instead of upbraiding him for his persistence, as he expected her to (and he would have replied that he could not help it, because he was a brash American), she said, "I'd love to, Richard . . . but I already have lunch plans."

Tubbs bulled right in. "Hey, I'm a social being. How about if I just tag along?"

She considered, then rejected this. "I don't think the man I'm meeting would go for that."

She had, however, remembered Tubbs' name, and he took that as a four-point advantage. Off her look, he said, "Whoever this guy is, he's making me powerfully jealous. Don't commit yourself to him until you get to know me a little better!"

She laughed at this. "Okay. How about dinner?"

"If you could handle the juggling act, I'd love to." There was no way he would turn her down, he thought, feeling the strong pull emanating from her. Speaking of juggling acts, how did this woman manage to juggle a classroom of cute kids with Calderone's globe-hopping? Then again, Mendez had said that Calderone had one in every port.

Almost seductively, she said, "Seven-thirty." At least, it seemed seductive to Tubbs. And despite his blood mission, his body was telling him that this woman wanted him, that she was on the level and on his wavelength, and that the odd feelings cropping up inside were no sham.

He nodded. She did not have to repeat the time of what would be their first social meeting.

And still she lingered in the hallway. Perhaps she'd been thinking of him since their meeting yesterday, too.

"Really, thank you so much for this." She indicated the watch.

He smiled brilliantly. "It's a pleasure. You're welcome."

He watched her return to the classroom. Then he hiked back to town, glad that no one was observing him, since he felt a bit light-headed and sappy.

Crockett would scoff, he knew. But the damned game was getting real.

—13—

TUBBS was strolling home along a stretch of back road that was mostly beach land bordering some large sugar-cane fields. A hired car, a plain white sedan, pulled to the shoulder; and he saw Crockett was at the wheel. He ran to catch up, climbed in, and Crockett pulled a one-eighty and headed back into town.

Music from one of the island radio stations floated out of the car on the salt breeze. "Thought you had a lunch date," Crockett began.

"Thought you weren't gonna spy on me, slick," Tubbs returned.

"It's not spying. I'm looking out for the welfare of my partner." It was the usual broadly played Sonny Crockett rejoinder.

"Yeah, well, for your information, it got moved up to dinner," said Tubbs. "And for another thing . . ."

He hesitated, clearly troubled. Crockett noticed. "I . . . I just don't know about this Angelina, man . . ."

"You mean something like, you can't see her as the mistress of a cop-killing sleazebucket like Calderone?"

"Something is wrong with it, Sonny. . . . I mean, I watched her with those kids. She's wonderful. And using her to get to Calderone is starting to make me feel . . . wrong."

Crockett tried to sound like the voice of experience. "Backpedal a bit, Tubbs. Remember that you haven't been with us for long, and the police experience you had before had very little to do with role-playing. I've been doing it for over ten years . . ."

Tubbs cut in. "And you're now hard-shelled enough that you don't mind using people."

"Wrong, amigo. You never get used to it."

This surprised Tubbs. "Yeah?"

"Just because this chick Angelina is playing *The Sound of Music* with you doesn't mean she isn't just as good at another act when she's with Calderone." His voice a bit harder, Crockett added, "Don't go gettin' turned around here, buddy."

"Hey, nobody has to tell me about getting turned around," Tubbs snapped. "I know exactly what we came here for. Buddy. So how'd you make out?"

"Academy Award time," Crockett boasted. "I put them up against the wall for an extra thirty grand. We should be hearing from the Calderone Zone by late this afternoon."

Crockett slowed the car. The windshield had filled up with the rear end of a lumbering farm truck, a flatbed ringed with white pickets and stuffed with people. From a distance, Crockett had assumed they were farm laborers, but up close he and Tubbs saw to their surprise that they were costumed villagers—all dancing in the tight space, swigging wine, puffing *ganja,* and having a grand old time. The bizarre papier-mâché getups lent a surreal air to the encounter; the utterly mundane surroundings clashed with the truckload of dancing goat-men and bat-women and garishly painted demons. Some of the revelers beat on skin drums or piped wind instruments. As Crockett and Tubbs pulled up to their tailgate, they turned to notice, shouting and waving hysterically in various dialects.

Tubbs cracked a smile. "Party people. On their way to de Junkaroo, *mon.*" He waved back and made a face. He was rewarded with overdone, pantomimic reactions from the revelers.

"Yeah," grumbled Crockett, "and they're going at a crisp five miles per hour." He swung the car into the far lane to pass and was greeted by the elephant bellow of an oncoming truck moving at a considerably faster clip. The truck's burly driver laid on the horn and shook his fist, but did not cut his speed. Crockett tucked the car back in behind the Junkaroo truck as the oncoming vehicle blew past. A small blue Chevy covered with gray primer dutifully fell into line behind Crockett on the congested roadway.

Tubbs stiffened in his seat from the close call. "Careful, son—I'm not quite ready to become anybody's hood ornament just yet."

"Those jokers behind us sure are."

Tubbs turned to look just as the blue Chevy darted

out, piling up speed to pass, moving parallel to them in the next lane. The Chevy was filled with more festival-goers who waved frantically at Crockett and Tubbs. There were four of them, wearing masks suggestive of skulls, devils, and reapers.

Crockett rolled his eyes and returned a halfhearted wave; then the two skull-faces on the starboard side of the car lifted submachine guns and began blasting away at the rental car. Crockett stomped on the brakes just as the first salvo of bullets tore apart their left front fender. At the same time, his right arm struck out to jerk Tubbs down beneath the line of fire. But Tubbs had already hit the deck.

The blue Chevy, still in the far lane, dropped speed and slid back into view. The low, nasty, burping noise of bullets vibrated the air, and the windshield assumed a crushed-ice pattern right before Crockett's eyes. Only about half the partygoers in the truck ahead of them had noticed what was going down; the others were still dancing.

Crockett put his fist through the windshield, punching out a hole big enough to see through, then gave the car some gas, causing it to lurch ahead and avoid the next burst.

He tossed his .45 heavily into Tubbs' lap. "Shoot at these bozos, willya? I've gotta drive this thing."

Slugs disintegrated the rear-deck windshield, and Tubbs flinched. Then he leaned over the seat and gave the Chevy four well-placed shots that caused the attack car to drop back.

"Hang on!" Crockett floored it and zipped around the Junkaroo truck, blind. They lucked out and did not meet the grilles of any oncoming vehicles. But the blue Chevy clung to their tail, pulling up behind the truckload of revelers and preparing to pass.

Tubbs had not brought along his own hardware: he'd assumed he wouldn't need it for lunch with Angelina. The rest of their arsenal was still stowed in Crockett's speedboat under lock and key. Sonny unsnapped a fresh clip for the .45 and used it to knock away some more of the shattered windshield. Gemlike cubes of broken safety glass were all over them.

"We're coming into town," he said, placing the clip on the seat next to Tubbs.

"Yeah, and here comes company again." The blue Chevy swerved in front of the truck and poured on the acceleration. Tubbs fired through the rear window, and the car skidded like a shot deer, jumping over into the oncoming lane.

Signs blurred past. They were heading into the town at high speed. Buildings, pedestrians, more festival people began to whip by in fast-motion.

"Aw, what the hell is this?"

"People!" shouted Tubbs unnecessarily. "And cars! And . . . whoaaaa, no!"

Crockett hit the brakes and cranked the wheel hard, sluing sideways through a cobblestone intersection. "Hard right!" People dove for cover, their eyes saucer-size with abrupt panic, as the Chevy barreled in not far behind. Wild potshots knocked chunks out of the masonry.

Tubbs was shoved halfway across the seat by inertia, and climbed up to take a look out the rear window. "Still tied to our tail!" he shouted, squeezing off a luck shot that punched a quarter-size hole in the windshield of the Chevy. It swerved and took out a fruit stand, spraying apples and oranges and mangoes every which way . . . but did not drop speed.

Crockett's eyes stuck to the road, to the mirrors. It took all of his driving skill just to keep them from mashing some bystander flat, or becoming part of a wall, or flipping over. He cut another corner too close and bruised the right rear wheel against a high curbing. The bump slammed Tubbs' noggin against the ceiling of the cabin.

"We gotta get outta this city!" Crockett exclaimed seriocomically.

Hot lead keened off their rear end, scratching sparks off the chrome and killing both taillights in little bursts of colored plastic. Crockett corner-cut another curve and headed in the direction of the oceanfront. Tubbs kept the chase car back a block or so by emptying the automatic's clip, then reloading.

A berobed Junkaroo celebrant wearing an enormous papier-mâché steer's head turned just in time to see the chewed-up rental car careening wildly toward him. Before he could get center-punched, he leapt, grabbing for a rain gutter. He made it, but his oversize head didn't. Tubbs felt it crunch beneath their wheels.

"Sorry!" he shouted out the hole where the passenger window used to be. The man shook his fist in response, then had his hands full trying to dodge the bullets flying from the blue Chevy. The smashed bull-head vanished under its front bumper.

"Crockett! The flower stand!"

"I see it, I see it!" He hit it anyway, as he jigged

to the right to avoid a running child who was not sufficiently aware of the threat presented by moving automobiles. Fresh blooms filled the air behind them and rained down on the chase car, pattering off the roof and hood.

"Crockett—this is a dead end!"

"It better not be!" They were headed for a judicial, columned building at sixty miles an hour. Terrified citizens ran up the steps to evade the oncoming car.

Crockett spotted an alley and hooked into it. Its far end was barricaded by a slat fence. He drove through it.

"They still with us?"

"Like a bad dream," said Tubbs, watching the Chevy clear the gap they'd just made in the fence.

This time they encountered a dead end for real, and had to pull a high-speed three-sixty. For a scary moment, the rental and the chase were swapping shots directly, like gunfire between horses on opposite sides of a merry-go-round. Then Crockett raced back the way they'd come.

"Left!" shouted Tubbs.

"Right," said Crockett, agreeing.

"No. Left!"

The left turn pointed them toward the docks again. A small harbor flew by. Fishermen looked up to see what the shooting was about.

Like a locked-on, heat-seeking missile, the blue Chevy reappeared in their wake.

Disgusted, Crockett said, "Hang on Tubbs—I'm gonna *park* this thing!"

At top speed he turned right onto the pier. The

old salts and tourists lining the pier were too surprised to react. They merely gawked . . . as the car ran out of pier and took to the air.

"Can you swim?" yelled Crockett as they went nose-first into the sea.

Seawater plumed upward on both sides and gushed in freely, breaking away the rest of the front windshield. Then Tubbs heard the horrible *glurk* of underwater sound as the car quickly took on more water and sank, its tail jutting into the air.

The Chevy stopped near the pier and the assassins piled out. Guillermo Pino ripped away his devil mask to take better aim. The other men followed his lead and exhausted their clips at the sinking car. The gas tank was a perfect target, thanks to the angle, and soon the slugs found it. There was a flat, hollow boom that echoed off the buildings. Pieces of the car spun up into the air, and a flaming halo of gasoline burned on the surface of the water. The blown-off trunk lid was the only part still visible after the rest of the car was totally immersed. All that was left were flames and oil smoke. Pino nodded approvingly and waved his men back to the Chevy. The sounds of sirens pierced the air from a distance.

Tubbs released the reeds growing from the bottom of the bay and kicked himself upward, toward the sunlight. His lungs were bursting, starved for air, but he made it. Treading water as well as spitting it, he rubbed his eyes and saw that he was twenty yards from the flaming gasoline. The blaze was petering out. Many concerned people were staring at him, but none had that lifeguard look.

Crockett's Panama hat floated past his nose, filling him with sudden panic.

"Crockett!" He did a full circular sweep. "Sonny!"

With a strangled, gurgling noise, Crockett broke the surface ten feet away. He sucked air and spluttered.

"Sonny!"

Hocking the horrible salt taste out of his mouth, Crockett said, "Present."

"I think we just heard from Calderone."

"Yeah, but who was he calling on—you or me?"

It was a small island, as Chief Albury had said. The attack might have been prompted by Calderone in response to the attention Tubbs was directing toward Angelina, or it might have been a simple and direct response to "Miller"'s demand for more pay.

Or . . . it might have been a third, more deadly possibility.

Suddenly there were uniformed officers all over the pier. Two such men cast off in a small skiff to retrieve Crockett and Tubbs; and in ten minutes they found themselves toweling off, courtesy of Chief Albury.

"I just received word of what happened," he said, concerned half for their safety and half for all the damage they had caused. "Are the both of you all right?"

"Barely," said Tubbs sourly, ruffing his hair with the soaked towel.

Albury considered the smoking oil slick on the

water, all the onlookers, and the two drenched vice cops. "I was on my way to your hotel when my radio filled up with news of a wild chase through the city streets. Reckless driving and gunshots . . ."

Crockett cut him short. "Did you have something for us? Any new leads?"

Albury nodded grimly. "One of our sources, an island man named Red Tulle, reported that Calderone's yacht departed from the island. His sighting was later verified by my assistant here, Mr. Henderson."

Henderson, a young, bright-eyed understudy to Albury, stepped forward to be recognized.

"How long ago?" Crockett snapped.

"This morning. Calderone's yacht registry is number seven-sixty-eight–alpha–three-eleven, signed to a Macedonian holding company. It is his boat."

Crockett and Tubbs exchanged a look of shrinking hope. "That's one of Calderone's corporate fronts," Tubbs noted.

Henderson, eager to add something, said, "We put in immediate calls to the closest neighboring islands as soon as we came by this intelligence. A yacht fitting the description came into San Marcos around noon, for refueling."

That had been approximately when Tubbs found the path winding up toward the schoolhouse—which meant the police did not have their timing off. Angelina had not left with Calderone. "Why didn't you guys call in the Coast Guard?"

"Spotter planes were alerted," said Henderson.

"Unfortunately," said Albury, "there is a good

five thousand square miles of open sea out there, and his destination was unknown. He could have charted a course for Cuba, the Antilles, Costa Rica..."

"Damn it!" Crockett was getting sick of Albury's cheery tourist statistics.

"I feel responsible," Albury continued, looking sadly at the mess. "We did nothing to avert this situation."

"Don't," Crockett muttered.

"If there's anything we can do for you while you remain on St. Andrews Island..."

Crockett interrupted him. "I appreciate it, chief, but Tubbs and I will be going back to Miami right away."

This was news to Tubbs.

"Fine," said Albury. He seemed satisfied, even pleased, as though Crockett had answered a test question correctly. "Henderson will naturally arrange a ride back to your hotel for you."

"We can walk it from here," said Crockett.

Albury nodded officiously. "Again, my deepest apologies for... for all of this." He appeared genuinely shocked and affected. He rendered a little half-bow and then moved off with Henderson trotting behind.

Tubbs was steaming, near the flash point. "That's it? We just pick up bag and baggage and split?"

"Shh! Cool it," Crockett said *sotto voce*, pretending to be interested in the ocean. He watched until Albury's car started and moved off. The gawkers were dispersing. "This stinks."

Moving close, Tubbs lowered his voice. "What are you talking about?"

"Coincidence. Convenience. The way the shooting just went down. I think Calderone has known who the hell we are ever since we checked in."

"How?" returned Tubbs. "Albury?"

"Give the New Yorker twenty-four silver dollars." Crockett seemed brutally enlightened and thoroughly ticked.

"How do you know?"

"He's the only one on the island who knows who we are. He didn't show up until the hitters in the car left the scene. *No* cops showed the whole time we were being chased. That's enough for me to assume that Albury is connected to Calderone. How about you?"

Tubbs nodded reluctantly. "That means no backup. No support. The police here are linked up with the bad guys. And our badges aren't even worth hock value."

"Joo got it, mang," Crockett said, recalling their old nemesis Trini de Soto. "We're so under, we might as well be on another planet."

"I'm going back to see Angelina—soon as I get some dry clothes. If Calderone really did leave, I think I can get a destination out of her."

Crockett eyed him for a moment. "That the only reason you want to see her?"

Tubbs' face assumed that peculiar flat look again. "Business," he said. Then, for the benefit of the stragglers who were still staring at them, he added, "Come on, let's go pack and get the hell out of here."

–14–

WITH a little help from the locals, Tubbs managed to find the address Angelina had given him earlier that day. *That* day—it rocked him to think that it had not yet been a week since he and Sonny were comfortably ensconced in the stakeout on Felix Castronova.

Tubbs had set out from the Conch Bay Lodge secure in the impulsive thought that Angelina liked him and would be straight with him. He needed no lies, and he had no time left for half-truths. By sheer earnestness, he thought he could convince her to help him find Calderone. The earnestness hearkened back to another gut-ache: the death of Rafael at Calderone's hands. But this *new* feeling had something to do with his gradual perception of Angelina. As powerful as Calderone was, Tubbs thought, surely he could be no more to this woman than a physical lover . . . ? An amorously inclined patron of her art studies, perhaps, who demanded more than paintings as payment for his financial aid . . . ?

Surely she felt nothing for someone like Calderone in return?

Another image that disturbed Tubbs was the scene at the schoolhouse. It didn't jell with the picture he had forged in his mind. He had always known hookers who could neatly divide their lives. You never suspected that the woman in Levi's and tennis shoes with whom you bumped carts at the supermarket was, by night, an encapsulation of your sexual fantasies in spike heels and leather. Tubbs knew Trudy Joplin and Gina Calabrese, and knew the unnervingly schizoid way in which they became prostitutes in the line of duty one moment, then changed masks and became vice cops just like him. The illusion had to be seamless . . . or they would've wound up dead long ago. So why was it so impossible for him to consider Angelina as a teacher by day and a sometime whore after sunset?

The vibrations were all wrong. Of the "sharks and weirdness" Tubbs had noted, half-jokingly, Angelina was becoming a major weirdness.

The winding, paved road was one car's width, encroaching as little as possible on the vegetation covering the hillside. It wandered ever upward, here and there exposing little turnoffs and private drives. There was an occasional streetside mailbox. The residences Tubbs could see past their shields against the outside world—labyrinthine driveways and entire forests of foliage—looked expensive and sprawling. Villas, mansions, estates.

Angelina's residence seemed even more costly to him because it was small—tucked away among the giants, a quiet home that made a rash statement of power through its own small existence. It was white stucco, laid out in an L-pattern with the porch and front door inside the crook of the L. In one wing, a turret rose above roof level. It looked rather like a walkup lighthouse, accessed from inside. On top of it, three-hundred-sixty degrees of windows took in everything on the hillside. Tubbs was sure that from that height there was a spectacular view of the ocean.

He pressed the doorbell and heard a soft gong chime within. This was soon answered by the softer sound of naked feet crossing a slate floor.

Angelina opened the door clad in two lush magenta bath towels, one wound around her body, the other turbaned around all of her hair. Droplets of water clung to her long neck.

If it was a fake, thought Tubbs, it was a damned good one. Her face seemed to bloom upon seeing him.

"A little early for dinner, yet," she said wryly.

"Angelina . . . something's come up," he began as soberly as he could. "I've got to leave the island in a couple of hours."

Disappointment flitted across her face. "But . . . so soon, Richard?"

"Business. On the mainland. Urgent. Important. It has to do with . . ." He trailed off. "Listen, I have to talk to you."

She stood aside. "Come in. Please." When he was inside, she closed the door.

Tubbs was losing it, fumbling. There was no way she'd buy the story about Calderone. Nevertheless, he had to try. "This is . . . a difficult thing for me to say—"

She overrode him. "No. I understand. I've been feeling the same way, too."

Her arms slid around his neck and she moved close. Tubbs' brain slammed from thirty to ninety in one second. She had misinterpreted his awkwardness as a prelude to a romantic confession—and now she was holding him, her maddeningly clean scent fogging his mind. Tubbs felt instantly intoxicated.

But his arms enclosed her, burrowing into the humid dampness of the bath towel. "Feeling what way?"

"Ever since I met you yesterday." She gently pulled his head down to meet her lips, and Tubbs closed his eyes. First contact was electric; it seized him from inside and obliterated everything else. "There," she said, "that wasn't so hard." Then his vision filled up with her face again. She leaned backward in his careful embrace, and the towel unwound from her hair to pool on the floor. Tubbs moved his hands into its glossy blackness.

"You trust me," Tubbs said, deeply moved inside, as well as by the passion of the moment.

Ingenuously, innocently, she said, "Why shouldn't I?" He saw the pupils of her eyes widen, drinking in his image. They were both triggered now, and stood there for an age, holding each other and exploring.

At last she pulled away just far enough to indicate the wrought-iron staircase that wound up inside of the turret section of the house. She led him by his hand. Halfway up the stairs, she left the other towel behind.

Jimbo Spitz blew lustily into his harmonica, valving it with his hand into a violent, ragged blues riff. He grooved mightily on his own sound, then stared up at Crockett from his gargoyle-like perch on the bungalow's porch railing. Crockett was packing up his seabag.

"You sure you hombres gotta ride off inta the sunset?" Jimbo asked, giving another blast. "Junkaroo's what you call your *major* power party, man. We're gonna be dropping some primo windowpane. Just came in from Oakland this morning with a college prof from Berkeley."

"Sounds tempting, Jimbo," Crockett said, half sarcastically, "but I just don't get the kick I used to from turning my brains into boiled squash." He thought of Elvis, freaking out at the odd sudden movement as though ducking invisible monsters only he could see, or floating through the now-and-then murky reptilian LSD flashback.

"Hey, bud, don't get me wrong," Jimbo protested, "this isn't recreational tripping."

"Strictly spiritual, right?" He had heard this one before.

"It helps my writing. Check this out—

"Parallel lines trail off into
The sun's blinking eye while
We eat mangoes from a dying carcass.
Come back to the five and dime . . . Zarathustra."

"I'm stunned," Crockett said. "What is that—Moody Blues played backwards?"

Proudly, Jimbo said, "It's from *Nylon Truth.*"

"Which is?"

"My first book of poetry for the masses. Verse for the people. Not that overcomplicated stuff like Rod McKuen does. This is more like . . . well, William Burroughs meets Stanley Kubrick."

"Must've missed out on that one," Crockett said. "I'll try to catch the film." He spotted some activity down at the docks and grabbed his field glasses for a look. What he saw froze him for just a second. It was Guillermo Pino, Calderone's one-eyed hit man, climbing from a small blue Chevy with dabs of gray primer and stepping onto a boat. He passed a bill to the dock attendant, who was finishing fueling the speedboat. Pino then kicked the monster into gear and blew away from the dock in a heavy backwash of white foam.

Jimbo was still rattling on about his book of poems. "It's not published yet, but I've got a couple of big agents in Pittsburgh real interested in it. We're still feeling each other out, understand . . ."

Crockett was not listening. "Right."

Jimbo noticed his tight expression. "Hey man, you copa? You look like you just saw Jim Morrison or something." He pocketed his harp.

"Yeah. I'm real copa." Crockett turned and dug out some cash. "Jimbo, I think I've changed my mind. Run into the village and see if you can scare up a couple of Junkaroo masks for Tubbs and me."

"For tonight?"

"You got it." He was still looking toward the

dock. The speedboat had receded to a tiny white speck. It could only have one destination.

"Far *out!* I knew I could talk you dudes into partyin'! You won't regret this, man."

And Jimbo was gone. Crockett wondered how Ricardo Tubbs was making out.

The pressure of her lips was soft and fragrant, and she withdrew to snuggle in beside him—one arm around his head, the other caressing the musculature of his bare chest. Tubbs was no Schwarzenegger, but he had his physical virtues.

Angelina's were obvious.

They lay side by side in her bed. The sheets were dark blue and were now lightly dappled with sweat. The circular room was brilliant with light from the windows—plus the conical peak of the turret itself, which housed two wide skylights. Tubbs' clothing, for the most part, was draped over the wrought-iron bannister leading up to this timeless and, for him, magical little room.

He felt fully charged and at ease in spirit, for one of the first times since venturing from New York on his mission of vengeance. He cradled her in his arms and meditated on the moment, drawn back to the present only by the sound of her voice.

"Who are you, Richard?"

Questions like that tended to kick Tubbs immediately into a defensive mode. "What do you mean?"

"Do you always answer questions with questions?"

Smiling at her, he said, "Do I seem like that kind of person to you?"

Another kiss, another long pause.

"I watch your eyes," she said. "And sometimes, I can see your mind drifting to other places—places where others are never allowed. Not necessarily pretty places. Your eyes say you can give so much of yourself, but you resent other people trying to give to you."

This revelation struck Tubbs, and he did not like being probed so openly. *Why would she say things like that,* he thought, *unless . . . ?* "My problems aren't worth going into," he said.

"Unless somebody cares," she returned. "Don't you understand?"

Against his better nature, his ingrained defense mechanisms moved to divert her. "Didn't I tell you?" he said lightly, afraid to even consider the reason he'd come up here in the first place. "I'm just one of the world's great misunderstood souls."

"No, come on, really."

"Well, I see something in your eye, too."

Enthralled—and diverted—she said, "Do you?"

"Yeah. A little, tiny eyelash, right here . . ." He reached to pluck the stray, and she laughed.

"You goof. Hand me the brush."

He looked around himself dumbly. *"Donde está?"*

She pointed. He lifted a flimsy Oriental chemise from the night table and picked up the silver brush beneath it. Then his eyes spotted something else on the bedstand.

It was an oval portrait shot of Angelina. She must have been all of seventeen. She was smiling lovingly and had her arms wrapped around an equally beaming man: Francisco Calderone, his hair a little darker but otherwise the same.

Tubbs saw the truth highballing toward him like a runaway freight train; yet, he fought to avoid it. He picked up the gilded frame and tried to joke it away. "Don't tell me we were being spied on by your boyfriend this whole time?" he said. "Isn't this guy a little bit old for you?"

She smiled in genuine pleasure, sitting up in the bed to brush her damp hair. "He's not too old to be my father."

He had to pull energy from deep inside to keep his exterior cool. His chance to reveal all to her had blackened and rotted away in his hands. It was too late now. She'd think she was just being used. His brain reeled. This delicate creature had sprung from Calderone's loins? Now he saw why her features seemed to be a mix of aristocrat and low-born. If he looked hard enough into her face, he could even see vague hints of the man who had killed his brother. But he kept himself collected. "Your father—"

"I was hoping you'd decide to stick around for the Junkaroo," she said. "I wanted to introduce you two."

"Tonight?"

She nodded. "There's a Bal Masque at the beach club."

He sat up, grasping her shoulders. She arranged herself in his embrace and returned a long, deep kiss.

"How can I pass that up?" he said. "Things have changed, haven't they?"

That seemed to be just what she wanted to hear. "You'll have a wonderful time. *We* will."

"Right," he said bitterly. "I love masquerades."

–15–

"HIS *daughter!*" Crockett was unmanned and flabbergasted.

Tubbs had said the one thing that knocked the entire picture they had constructed of Francisco Calderone into skew. He was still having a tough time matching up Angelina with the man he had almost blown away, point-blank, in Miami less than two months ago. They held the same blood. Reality vertigo swam in and out for him; he was having difficulty staying businesslike.

"I'm meeting Calderone tonight at the Junkaroo festival," he said. "She insisted we meet; I didn't even do any prodding."

"I asked Jimbo to scare up some masks just to get him out of my hair," said Crockett. "Now I'm glad I did. It looks like we're gonna need 'em." The wheels of his mind ground up the new information, and he was off and planning while Tubbs paced around the room and finally slumped into a sling-back chair. "We'll pull out; make sure Albury's spotters in the harbor see us leave. Then we'll double back. We can dock down the coast in one of those hidden coves Albury is so fond of beefing about."

Tubbs was locked blackly into his own thoughts. He looked up to see Crockett studying him. "I care for this woman, Sonny." He couldn't put it any more straightforwardly. "As far as she knows, her father is just a wealthy financier who regularly donates half his income to the Catholic church. Very nebulous. He's done a great job of keeping her totally in the dark." He disliked how Angelina's existence corrupted the one-sided picture he had formed of Calderone—a picture that kept his hatred at a high flame. Before, the thought of blowing Calderone to smithereens had been pleasurable; Tubbs had thought thousands of times of jamming his brother's sawed-off shotgun into the sawed-off dope dealer's mouth and blasting his brains straight into Satan's lap. Now it wasn't so simple. To kill Calderone would be to crush the fragile, unique thing that was Angelina.

"You're really twisted out of shape by her, aren't you?" Crockett said. He understood.

That also gnawed at Tubbs. Crockett had saved his hide. And Calderone had tried to eliminate Crockett. Tubbs owed it not only to Rafael, but to Sonny to bring Calderone down. But it hurt him now, just the same. Impotent with fury, he said, "Why can't it ever be black and white? You go after the bad guy, and you either get him or he gets you;

and that's the finish. How come innocent people have to get destroyed in the process . . . ?"

He already knew the answer to that one. Life was not plotted so neatly as most bad movies. And innocence was no longer a privilege . . . it was a crime. You were innocent; you got burned by the world, which never gave a damn.

"You changing your tune about scooping up Calderone," asked Crockett point-blank, "or what?"

"Absolutely not." There—it was out, for better or worse. He was committed. He felt right. He also felt as if he might just throw up sometime real soon.

Someone, at least, was in a little higher spirits. Footsteps approached the bungalow, followed by off-key jive-ass singing. *"Ah-know Ah-know . . . I know* she's a country girl!" High was right: high as a kite, Jimbo Spitz breezed over the porch rail bearing two large shopping bags. *"Saaay,* let the good times roll, gents!"

"You got something for us?" said Sonny.

Jimbo's eyes were happily glazed. "Hey, would I let my Yankee brothers down? You guys are gonna be knee-deep in party-rama tonight, man." He delved into one bag, and with a flourish yanked out a garish papier-mâché demon face with painted white fangs. He looked Tubbs up and down. "This one is you. Totally!"

Tubbs tried it on while Crockett dug out a couple of twenties to grease Jimbo's palm.

"That's Seiloth," said Jimbo. "One of the Old Ones. He signifies Chaos."

"Thanks bunches," said Tubbs. "I feel pretty chaotic already."

"And for you, bwana," Jimbo said to Sonny, producing the other mask, "we have Dietrachboelet. Signifying Destruction. Powerful freakin' mojo, dudes. You will have major vibrations on the astral, you know."

"Chaos and Destruction," mused Crockett. "A great comedy double bill."

Like perfectly timed cinema thunder, somebody set off a string of party firecrackers as Crockett spoke.

"Don't scoff at the Old Ones," Jimbo said, so deadly serious it was funny. "They have great powers." He pocketed the bucks.

Crockett stowed his mask in his seabag. "Thanks, Jimbo. If we don't see you at the festival, take care of yourself."

They shook hands. "You dudes ever need to kick back, you know where to find me." He slipped an enormous bomber joint into Crockett's shirt pocket, then did likewise for Tubbs. "My dark brother," he intoned, "I'll see you on the Twenty-Fourth Plane."

"Just remember me when you get famous," Tubbs said.

Jimbo saluted them both and weaved off toward the nearest party. Twilight tinted the sky.

They shouldered their seabags and battened down Sonny's speedboat. As they were preparing to leave, Tubbs noticed Henderson sitting in a parked official car, making a radio call.

"I think we're being reported on," he said.

"To hell with him," said Sonny, kicking on the massive twin engines. They left Albury's constituency eating their spume.

Crockett put a few miles between them and the island, then cranked hard to port. "Let's set up," he shouted to Tubbs, who broke open the seabags.

He was considerably less ill at ease with the movement of the boat on the ocean this time. He sat calmly loading clips for Crockett's .45 automatic, which he handed over. Then he tossed Crockett a small Walther .38 in an ankle holster. He snapped open his mean little shotgun and slotted in two shells of high-velocity shot. He pocketed four more shells, then squirmed into a shoulder holster. He pulled a gleaming, blue-steeled .44 Magnum and knocked out the cylinder. After a moment he loaded it with blunt-nosed, pancaking wadcutter slugs.

Crockett noticed. "We're not going after a damned elephant, Tubbs."

By the time they were set up, darkness had enveloped most of the island. Crockett docked the boat inside the pocket of a black cove near the location Angelina had given Tubbs for the beach club.

Tubbs slipped on his demon mask. "It's party time," said Chaos.

He noted with amusement that Crockett, his friend, the vice cop expert at playing roles in deep cover, was comically inept at the art of simple Halloween-style masquerade. "Those white shoes and that walk of yours would give you away anywhere," he told Crockett.

"I feel like I should be sticking up a liquor store with this thing on," Crockett replied from behind his Destruction mask.

They were standing near the conflagrant glow of a bonfire in the middle of the club's private beach. Steel-drum music filled the air; barefoot revelers in grotesque masks danced around them and shared drinks. Many of them drank through straws, so as to preserve their secret, masked identities.

The beat pounded away at reality. The thumping of goatskin drums blended with the jangling of herd bells, the toot-honk of raucous horns, the ratcheting of noisemakers. Earth-animal partygoers carried one another off to cavort in the darker dunes of sand. The far end of the beach was anchored by a second billowing, sparking bonfire; and between the two snaked a colorful, sense-staggering conga line. Horns blared. Whistles keened in countertime to the jungle beat. Anything that could be pressed into service as a rhythmic instrument—empty cans, bottles, even the masks themselves—was accordingly pounded, stroked, or tapped. Even without a drink or a puff or a pop, it was an intoxicating scene. A lizard demon juggled three flaming torches. A giant chicken did magic tricks. Some revelers tossed away their clothing in abandon.

Destruction stood in his characteristic Sonny Crockett pose and surveyed the scene. "See the girl yet?"

An artfully masked woman with legs very much like Angelina's wound her way toward them. A dancer vaulted madly and squatted in the masked woman's path, entreating her. They joined and whirled away in a frenzied dance, laughing.

"We're supposed to meet near the barbeque pit," said Chaos, in Tubbs' voice.

Another woman who could have been Angelina boiled out of the crowd and walked toward Tubbs, then continued past him without a nod.

"I don't like this," Tubbs said. "Too hard to tell the players."

"Wait a minute! Isn't that her? Over there?"

At the foot of the clubhouse steps, near a specially established beachside wet bar, Angelina removed an elaborately feathered mask and peered anxiously into the crowd, looking for Tubbs.

"Yeah," said Tubbs. "Back me. I might be looking at Calderone any second now."

"You're flanked," said Sonny. "I'll be watching your back. Play it normal and straight."

Crockett angled away into the throng while Tubbs walked over. Angelina held out her hands to greet him; the clasp melted naturally into an embrace. Then another wild conga line stomped past, momentarily cutting Tubbs off from view.

After a sustained kiss, Tubbs said, "Your father—is he here yet?"

She shook her head. "He's never anywhere on time."

"I'm looking forward to meeting him." It was unfair. He was setting her up and he knew it.

"Rraaahhhh!" A gruesome devil-dancer leapt down from the stairs, startling them both. They laughed. The demon did a few odd contortions, then capered gleefully away to scare others.

The steel band shifted tempo, and Angelina grabbed Tubbs, spinning him into an island dance. She put her mask back on. Over her shoulder, Tubbs could see Crockett lingering near the bar.

She clung tightly to him. "I wish we could just stretch out this moment into forever."

"So do I." He really meant it, too, considering what was about to happen.

Crockett watched them dance. Apparently Calderone was going to take his time showing up. This time, he didn't want any mistakes. He reached under his mask and popped a low-grain Dexamyl capsule—a holdover habit from his more dissipated days. He needed the edge the speed would give him. If he got too wired, he could leaven it with alcohol. Not the healthiest way to force a physical advantage, but certainly the quickest and most efficient emergency procedure he could think of. His mind kept replaying the way it had gone down in the Miami warehouse where they'd cornered Calderone before. If they'd been five minutes quicker on a jail pickup, Calderone wouldn't have dragged a judge out of bed and forked over the bail money.

"Hey mon," said a voice behind him, "Tubbs sent me." Expecting to see Jimbo Spitz, Crockett turned as the barrel of a revolver cozied up against his spine. "You don't want to live in a wheelchair," continued the voice, "walk slow and easy toward the bonfire."

Crockett was herded toward the beach. His keeper was a man whose identity was concealed behind a tight-fitting frog mask. Soon they left the revelers in the mid-distance and came to a little dock down by the ocean.

"Detective," said a familiar voice in greeting.

Crockett pulled off his mask. Chief Albury stood spread-legged in the sand, flanked by a pair of masked men holding guns aimed at Crockett. Nobody could see them at this distance.

Albury stepped forward and removed Crockett's .45 from its holster. Then Crockett was patted down from behind and relieved of the .38 strapped to his ankle. The gunman removed his mask and kept his own piece pressed into Crockett's left kidney.

"Pino," said Crockett. "I should've recognized the cheap shoes."

"Mr. . . . Miller." Pino nodded, his eyes cold and unblinking, like a cobra's.

"I'm sorry," Albury said in his usual syrupy, officious tone. "You should have left the island as you said you were going to. Now you no longer have any option."

"Thanks for your help," Crockett said. He wondered if they'd made Tubbs yet.

"Can I get you something to drink?" Tubbs was parched from dancing, and thought the mulled wine would go down as smooth as a kiss.

"Now that would be wonderful," she agreed.

It was a partial ruse. Calderone had not yet shown, and Tubbs had lost sight of Crockett. The trip to the bar might help him spot either of them. "Be right back."

While Tubbs stood at the bar, the frogman—Guillermo Pino—fell into place behind him. He pulled out his gun and pressed it into Tubbs' back.

"No problems," said the voice, low and unflappable. "Move. Come along with me."

A spaced-out Rastafarian waving a bottle interceded, almost by accident. "No violence, mon," he exclaimed, seeing the gun but not fearing it. "You gotta drink de rum!"

As the Rasta held up the bottle and the frogman turned to shove him away, Tubbs pivoted, grabbing the bottle and breaking it across the broad nose of the mask. Pino was momentarily blinded by broken glass and a spray of rum into his eyes.

Tubbs brought his foot sharply up; Pino woofed and bent double. Then Tubbs kicked the frogman in the face, causing the mask to implode with a crunch. Pino's gun flip-flopped away to land in the sand; he arched backward and fell in a spread eagle, out of gas.

"Too much rum," Tubbs said to the mildly shocked barman. The Rasta wandered away. There would be other hunters in the crowd, now that he'd been recognized.

There was no more time, and so much to do.

Tubbs hurried back to Angelina, grabbing her hand and pulling her through the crowd.

"Richard! What is it?"

Silent, determined, he moved. He could use some excuse to get her to where they'd hidden the cigarette boat, and then tell her the truth. He had to get some of the burden off his soul, and he did not have much time.

Two masked figures pulled their guns out and converged on them. Tubbs pulled Angelina through a conga line; the gunmen were efficiently sucked into that web of drinking and dancing, their chase confounded.

He felt as though he was pulling Angelina toward their common doom, and he despised it.

* * *

A quarter of a mile offshore, in the blackness of the nighttime ocean—the only reference points being the distant beach fires and the running lights of faraway-anchored pleasure craft—he throttled the cigarette boat to a stop.

While they drifted gently, he told her the truth. The truth was not going to make her free.

She sat in the passenger seat holding his badge limply in one hand. She did not look at him.

"A game," she said, breaking the terrible silence that had fallen between them. "The whole time . . . you were just using me." Her eyes did not redden or swell; there was no buildup to the pain. Tears simply started falling out. Her voice did not crack. Lines glistened on both her cheeks.

"Angelina . . ." His voice choked up. "That's not how it is."

Her dull shock evolved into rage in an instant, and she backhanded Tubbs smartly across the face. He sat there and took it. Defiance shone through the tears in her eyes.

"What kind of a person are you!" she yelled at him.

"You're not listening to me," he said, conscious that these were his exact words to Sonny in the hospital corridor when he was trying to keep him from strolling out and getting killed. "This is eating me up inside! I feel for you like I haven't felt for any woman in *years!* But I don't have any time to wrestle with my conscience now. I don't want to *lie* to you, Angelina. That's why I'm telling you these things! You've got to take me to your father!"

"You can go to hell," she spat.

"Your father kills people—and he's got my partner."

Their voices echoed across the water.

"My father is not a killer! Don't you think I know my own father!" She pushed him back.

Now Tubbs was getting mad. "For God's sake, why don't you open up your *mind* and your *eyes!* He's wanted in five countries!"

"No!"

"He's been an international crime figure for the past twenty years!"

"I don't believe you!" She slammed her hands over her ears as though she were being tortured.

Tubbs pulled a fistful of documents from the starboard locker and brandished them. "Arrest files! Francisco Calderone: possession with intent to sell a hundred and twenty kilos of cocaine! Car bombs! Assassination! Hit lists!"

"That's a lie!" she screamed at him.

"Yeah? Look at these: DEA files dating all the way back to 1966! You were seven years old! Photographs. You remember these gentlemen, don't you?" He threw the pictures at her viciously. "Trini de Soto, sex offender and hit man! Leon de Santis! Here's somebody you'll know—Rudolpho Mendez! Curly-haired fella, stops by the villa every now and then for a social drink? Leaves with a stuffed envelope?"

Her eyes flickered over the pictures, not wanting to recognize the familiar faces. Tubbs watched the slow horror creep into her face.

"I don't know what you're talking about!" But

she did. She was less emphatic; the sight of the pictures drained some of her fire.

Tubbs pressed on, acutely aware of how he was hurting her. "Mendez was kind enough to tell us about seven murders that your father had commissioned in Miami last month!"

"My father would never do that!" she shrieked in his face, spittle flying.

He screamed at her then, and the sound froze her. "Your father had a cop shot to death in New York City! *And that cop was my brother!*" Tears were coursing down his face now. The pain was a matter of dull nerve endings, as real as an open wound.

They stood locked in position, panting. She could scream no more. "I want to go now," she said quietly, as though dealing with a lunatic. "Just let me . . ."

"No," he said, his voice broken, "I can't."

"Please . . . leave me alone."

Fiercely resolute, he held her head in his hands and fixed her eyes. "Take me to him. I'll show you who and what your father really is."

He saw her sensing the truth and not wanting to face it. When she spoke, it was with grief for what had been lost, and had nothing to do with her father. "What does it matter, Richard?" she said. "What does it matter?"

–16–

THE floor of the villa's auditorium-size dining room was polished black slate so dark that it looked like a glossy pool of still water. The archwork was a classy, costly Art Deco design with chromium surfaces; and one wall was lined floor-to-ceiling with mirrors. The kidney-shaped dining table was a slab of solid glass two inches thick; the dinner service was done in clear crystal and sterling silver. Beyond the table were sliding glass doors; past those, an Olympic swimming pool whose water threw aquamarine reflections around the room. The sheer weights of glass and mirrors caught the highlights and tossed them around. The lighting was subdued, indirect, complemented by candles on chromium trees and floating oil-wick lamps.

The effect of the room was very unsettling. It

was cold, shining, soulless, with overtones of deadliness.

Francisco Calderone hacked apart a well-done filet mignon. He stuffed his face with little grace and gulped wine half a glass at a time. The wine provided one of the few spots of color in the entire room. It was the crimson hue of fresh blood.

Crockett found the tableau eerie, recalling the last time he'd seen Calderone—on the Miami docks where he and Tubbs had ambushed the dealer. Calderone had been surrounded by bodyguards then, as well. While the dope kingpin dealt indifferently with his expensive dinner, two sentries bearing machine guns stood to either side of his chair. A third lingered by Crockett, who was handcuffed.

The sliding doors were open, and the hot night air eddied into the cavernous room. Calderone's back was to the swimming pool.

"I'm looking forward to seeing Miami again," he said around a mouthful of food. "Nice scenery in that town, friendly people . . ." His Colombian bodyguards stood statue-still, their eyes on Crockett, ready to kill him at a wink from the short man with the wayward mustache.

"Miami's looking forward to seeing you," Crockett said in monotone. He was rewarded with a gun barrel bruising his ribs.

Calderone laughed derisively, a nasty, hacking sound. "You mean your local authorities?" he said, eyes glittering with a clear sense of his superiority. "Those bozos? For a C-note I got cops lined up to clean my toilet bowls." He dropped his fork on the table. The crash echoed in the sensitive acoustics of the metal and glass room.

He seemed wholly crazed, a madman with a volcanic temper ready to spurt through a barely maintained façade of humanity. Or perhaps, Crockett thought, he appeared insane because he was so removed from normal people and so intensely fixated. Ruefully, he thought, *so this is how the other half lives . . .*

"You don't get it, do you?" Calderone said to him. *"No comprende.* The DEA, FBI, city cops, county Vice . . . all the computers and technologies . . . they can't catch one little man who never made it past the fourth grade. You know something? The closest I ever get to a judge is when I tee off with them at the Luke and Dender Country Club. That's right; your bosses taught me how to play golf." He sniffed. "Too bad they didn't teach you anything."

Crockett's hands were cuffed in front of him. He tested his bonds. No go.

Contemptuously, Calderone rose, wineglass in hand, peering at Crockett over the rim as though toasting him. "Forty-two million dollars last year. Tax-free. That why they call it the land of opportunity?" He giggled.

"Even fat cats fry," said Crockett.

"Only when they allow mistakes to occur. You're a mistake. But it'll take much smarter cops than you. Look where you've wound up. What has it gotten you? *Nada.*"

Guillermo Pino strode briskly across the patio, entering through the dining room doors. He stood before Calderone until motioned to talk.

"Señor Calderone," he said submissively, not at all the stone-cold killer now. "The black one. He escaped. He . . ."

Calderone stared at Pino's face. It was bleeding. He was nursing a shiner around his left eye where Tubbs had kicked in his frog mask. He was scuffed up. Calderone's expression darkened; it was like watching a rolling thundercloud boil. Before Pino could say any more, Calderone smashed the empty wineglass into crystal fragments against the side of Pino's head.

Sparkling splinters sprayed. Pino slumped heavily to one knee, his ear nearly ripped off and spurting a freshet of blood. Furiously, Calderone kicked him and kicked him until Pino rolled up fetally. *"Idiota!"* he hissed through clenched teeth. *"Bastardo!* You worthless piece of garbage!"

Then he grabbed Pino and hauled him up. "Find him!" he raged into the dazed man's face. Then he shoved the man roughly out the door. Grateful to be alive, Pino humped away as fast as he could, limping.

Calderone's expression was almost casual when he turned back. Pointing at Crockett, he said to the two bodyguards, "Shoot him five times in the back of the head and dump him in the ocean." It was the trademark of a syndicate hit.

"Father . . . ?"

It was Angelina's voice, and it froze them all. She moved into the room, walking with almost trancelike slowness. She looked at the guards, and at Crockett. She looked at the blood and broken glass on the floor. And then she looked at Calderone.

He seemed annoyed. "Angel . . . what're you doing here?"

Scared now, she said, "Someone has . . . told me some things about you."

His brow creased. He was not in control. "Who have you been talking to?" He was unsettled.

"Me." Tubbs stepped out from the hallway behind her. He said the single syllable from behind the chopped-off twin bores of Rafael's customized shotgun.

Angelina was losing control of herself. Tubbs' whole rancid scenario was coming to life right before her eyes. She saw her father's reaction to Tubbs' presence and knew they had met before—and had not spent their time discussing the weather.

Crockett tensed. This was not going to be easy.

Tubbs' voice really carried in the hollow room. "Tell those goons of yours to drop their weapons right now—or I'll splatter your brains all over your silver service."

"What're you doing?" cried Angelina. "No!"

"Angelina, get out of here!" Tubbs snapped.

Calderone's eyes flew between them. "You heard him! Get out of here, now!"

She was disoriented, dangerously close to losing it. She took a tentative step toward him "Father . . . ?"

"Go!"

"Drop them," Tubbs told the bodyguards. "I mean it."

Calderone snapped his fingers once, twice. Both

men bent slowly, easing their weapons toward the floor.

Only Crockett saw what was going down. As the first man's gun touched the floor, the second brought his swiftly up into the firing line, cutting loose a short burst at Tubbs, who shoved Angelina violently out of the way. The salvo went wild as Crockett broadsided the shooter and the room filled up with the mega-amplified, reverberating racket of gunfire.

Bunching his fists, Crockett swung a wide roundhouse blow, flattening the nose of the shooter as the second man dove for his own weapon. The shooter fell back end-over-end atop a chair while Crockett went for the machine gun. Crockett doubted whether he could lift it and fire it with his hands cuffed.

As the second man spun to fire, Tubbs let him eat both barrels of the shotgun. A roar filled the room and obliterated all other sound; the bodyguard was blown completely out of his shoes and went twisting into the air to land atop the dining room table. He skidded all the way across, cleared away the remnants of Calderone's dinner, and collapsed in a broken jackstraw heap on the far side, leaving chunks of himself all the way over.

Calderone had clawed loose a silver-plated .45 automatic from beneath his suit coat and had drawn a bead on Tubbs' forehead. He fired his first round just as Tubbs took out the guard with the shotgun. Only the recoil knocked Tubbs clear by about half an inch; he felt the bullet sing past his forehead, and flinched.

Angelina was screaming. The gunshots drowned her out.

With a grunt, Crockett hauled the heavy machine gun off the floor, his finger groping for the trigger, the muscles in his hand twanging with pain.

Calderone dropped his arm back down and prepared to squeeze off the shot that would make Tubbs' head explode. Tubbs suddenly saw that Calderone would shoot through his own daughter if necessary to kill him. He also realized that he was weapons-naked. He dropped his empty shotgun and attempted a quick-draw of his .38. But Calderone had the lead.

The machine gun chuddered in Crockett's hand, the hard recoil kicking the barrel up toward the ceiling as he fired. Something in his wrist snapped like a broken rubber band.

The upward-tracking stream of slugs caught Calderone in the right hip and tore him apart in a crooked diagonal row of red holes up through his left shoulder. The shots continued ceilingward, blasting the glass doors into a billion singing pieces.

Calderone staggered backward. He stumbled through the glass doors as they fell apart and rained down on him. The shot he'd fired as he was hit went wild, destroying an oil-wick globe a foot away from Angelina's face. She fell to a huddle on the floor.

Swaying, his legs nonresponsive crutches, Calderone clumped in a drunken, lead-footed path toward the pool. He never made it. He turned halfway around to face Crockett and Tubbs, then sat down hard, his legs straight out in front of him. His mouth moved, but not a sound came out. The entire front of his body from the beltline up was slathered in pumping blood.

Then, quietly, he hinged backward. His head and one arm barely disturbed the surface of the water in the pool. Red liquid wisps began to seep out from them into the chlorinated water.

After that, the only sound was of Angelina's racking sobs.

—17—

CROCKETT felt gritty around the edges, with grains of gunk in his eyes and another Dexamyl pop thudding away in his bloodstream, destroying his appetite. He did not feel like eating anyway. The rays of the morning sun slammed into his head and booted his brains around; the coffee he was chain-drinking turned his stomach into a churning acid bath he could have developed photographs in.

He hated the administrative mop-up process. Why couldn't an inquest take as long as the shoot-out that prompts it, he wondered.

An investigating officer rolled up, notebook in hand. He wore a tropical-weight suit and a natty tie, and did not seem to know what perspiration was. He was talking to Crockett. Crockett could barely hear the man.

"Albury will be held in detention," the man was saying, "along with . . ."

"Henderson," said Crockett.

"Yes. Both will be held in detention until the preliminary hearing. We'll need both you and Detective Tubbs back here from the mainland sometime next week."

"You've got my number."

The investigator patted down his own pockets. "Ah . . . yes. Incidentally, you do know a Captain Swanson?"

"Yeah." Swanson, Sonny thought, was probably already caterwauling for a typewritten report.

"We received a message for you from him." He handed over a piece of paper folded into quarters. "Don't forget—next week."

"Right." Crockett wasn't particularly interested in Swanson's problems. He looked around for Tubbs.

A government Mercedes was parked conspicuously on the front lawn of Calderone's villa, the scene of the investigation. Close by, a second official held a clipboard and pocket recorder. He was asking Angelina Medera questions. She nodded, or shook her head, or answered with short sentences.

She wore a long, loose dress the gray of the center of a dove's eye. She looked businesslike, almost formal. Crockett felt sorry for her. All the inquiries about Calderone's financial holdings, all the dirty money and double dealing. She would tell them she knew nothing of it—and, because so many millions were involved, they would not believe her. Surely enough of Calderone's fortune was sheltered and legitimate—by now—to keep Angelina a wealthy woman for ten lifetimes. Her father's coke trade was the thick root of a sprawling above-ground business empire; and his board of directors and a cadre of expensive attorneys would see that it kept on turning a profit. But Crockett doubted if anyone would be eager to capture the throne Calderone had vacated last night—that of one of the world's principal movers and shakers in narcotics.

Tubbs stood nearby, not taking his gaze from Angelina. Every so often she inclined her head to look toward him. Her eyes were full of sorrow and brutal truth, but they also held for him a kind of pity.

Crockett dumped out his coffee and started on the cigarettes, thinking about how much he despised Styrofoam cups.

Perhaps the most tragic aspect was that the naive Angelina, the provocatively innocent one Tubbs had tried to stay in front of on the beach only a few days ago, had died along with her father. In her place was this more mature woman—harder, colder, more adult, less dreamy. And a little bit dead inside.

Just as the authorities would never believe she knew nothing of her father's connections, Angelina would never believe that Tubbs had been in love. Still was, Crockett judged, from his expression.

The cigarette boat was now moored to Calderone's private dock just below them, a two-minute walk away. Crockett thought of going home. Of sleeping, maybe for a week, on the *St. Vitus Dance* with the phone disconnected. Of waking up, maybe with his arm around Caroline . . . or Elvis. Of lying in the sun and burning off all the terrible things that had happened recently.

He saw Tubbs make his final move. Since he didn't want to watch, he turned his attention to Swanson's note.

Angelina headed for the open rear door of the Mercedes, but was aware enough of Tubbs' presence that she did not climb in. She spoke to the investigator, who moved discreetly out of range. Then she looked at Tubbs.

He moved closer, watching her face above the car's roof. She said nothing—merely stared at him as though she were examining him. Her expression was cold and uncharacteristic, almost studiously neutral.

"Angelina, I . . ." He faltered. "It wasn't supposed to turn out like this." His hands groped the air and tried to wrest some meaning out of it. Nothing made sense. All he could think of was the timeless interlude they'd spent together inside her secret lighthouse turret. And, for some strange reason, he kept remembering that her father had called her Angel.

Her eyes were locked with his now.

"I had it worked out," he said to her. "I *thought* I had it worked out. All except for you." He struggled with it; his voice hitched; and her stony silence did not make anything simpler. "I'm a cop, Angelina."

She smiled a sad, sardonic smile. "And that makes it okay for you, Richard?"

He winced as if stung.

"What brought you to this island, and to me, was something far more than just your job."

She ducked down into the car. The chauffeur gunned the motor and pulled smoothly away. Tubbs watched the car go until its last dust had settled.

He was aware of Crockett coming up on his right.

"You okay, buddy?"

Tubbs swallowed and forced a nod. "Yeah." They stood surrounded by officials and investigators, most of whom now ignored them. Their participation was over for the moment.

Crockett tapped out a cigarette, and Tubbs accepted it. Normally, he didn't smoke.

"I thought once this was done, I'd feel—I don't know—whole again," said Tubbs. "Like it would somehow make up for Rafael being gone forever. Like I had a Rafael-sized hole in me, and it would heal once we took care of Calderone. But the vengeance game doesn't work, Sonny. It just leaves you with another empty space inside. It's like a video game; you can't win. The only thing that matters is the degree to which you lose."

"Calderone slipped past us again, Tubbs," Crockett said, almost philosophically. "We all lose."

"I'm leaving a big piece of myself behind here," Tubbs said. "Almost as big as the one I left in New York. And you run out of pieces after a while, Sonny, y'know?"

Together they stared east. Another idyllic island day was beginning.

Crockett let out a long, soulful exhalation of smoke, and then waved the square of paper at Tubbs.

"Message from Swanson," he said. "Six hours old, almost."

"We're both fired," said Tubbs immediately.

"No. Rodriguez died in the hospital last night." His hand closed into a fist, wadding up the paper and dropping it on the manicured front lawn.

The news hit Tubbs like a forearm smash to the chest. He suddenly felt unable to breathe, and he saw Sonny was just barely maintaining. Rodriguez was gone. Rodriguez, who'd championed Tubbs and gotten him his Dade County shield. Lou Rodriguez, whom Crockett had looked up to as the most righteous of cops. Rodriguez with the terse orders, the limp clothes, and the smelly cigars.

No more.

It was Crockett who finally spoke. "C'mon—let's get the hell out of here and go home."

Tubbs cuffed him hard on the shoulder, as if to get him moving. "Yeah." Together they started down the slope, leaving behind some of the physical and emotional wreckage. Leaving behind Calderone's corpse in its zippered body bag—the symbol of something they'd grabbed for and missed.

They crossed the lawn and made for the dock. Ahead of them, the cigarette boat waited. Beyond that was the slowly rising sun, climbing up to its perch in the sky, and beyond that, Miami.